TIME TELLS ALL

CULLEN/BARTLETT DYNASTY BOOK 3

JANEEN ANN O'CONNELL

EVERYTHING HAS CHANGED

This book continues the journey begun in Book 2 (Love, Lies, and Legacies) of William and Margaret Blay. Despite the difficulties that plagued William and Margaret, their children, particularly their daughters, went on to lead productive, fulfilling lives, contributing to the Colony of Victoria.

In the stories of the characters in this book, I've tried to give voice to ancestors whose everyday achievements are often forgotten.

James Bryan Cullen and Elizabeth Bartlett, descendant chart

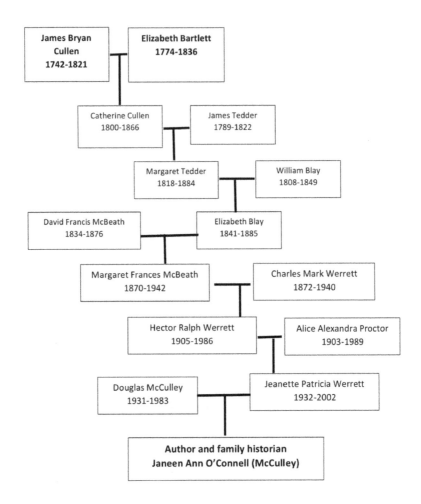

James Bryan Cullen 1742-1821

Elizabeth Bartlett 1774-1836

Catherine Cullen 1800-1866

James Tedder 1789-1822

Margaret Tedder 1818-1884

William Blay 1808-1849

David Francis McBeath 1834-1876

Elizabeth Blay 1841-1885

Margaret Frances McBeath 1870-1942

Charles Mark Werrett 1872-1940

Hector Ralph Werrett 1905-1986

Alice Alexandra Proctor 1903-1989

Douglas McCulley 1931-1983

Jeanette Patricia Werrett 1932-2002

**Author and family historian
Janeen Ann O'Connell (McCulley)**

AUTHOR'S NOTE

Their voices were stifled with the passing of time.

Their existence buried by succeeding generations. They are resurrected in the three books of the Cullen / Bartlett Dynasty

This is a work of historical fiction. I have tried to make historical facts accurate, but some incorrect items may have slipped through. With the tyranny of time, many records are hard to find. Marriages, deaths, births are as accurate as the available records indicate. I have used creative licence to fill in the gaps between birth and death.

Records were sourced from:

- Tasmanian Archives and Heritage Office
- University of Tasmania Library (www.utas.edu.au/library)
- Trove – National Library of Australia
- Public Records Office, Victoria
- State Library of Victoria
- Museums Victoria

ACKNOWLEDGMENTS

To the members of Melton Wordsmiths, thank you once again for critiquing my work and giving me valuable feedback.

To Melton Library and Learning Hub and Nicole Hilder, thank you for your support.

To members of the Melton Family History Group, thank you for challenging me to be historically accurate.

Once again, thank you, Robyn Hunter, for your editing expertise.

Thank you to Denise Wood for her uncompromising critiques.

This book is dedicated to the memory of my mother
Jeanette Patricia Werrett,
and her sisters:
Elaine Joan and Norma Ann

1

WILLIAM BLAY

Depression of the 1840s
"The Depression of the 1840s, experienced Australia-wide, was a major halt to rapid economic growth in Van Diemen's Land. The continued low price of wool in the London market after 1837, the 1839 English recession, the collapse of the mainland markets for grain and livestock, and the downturn of Tasmanian capital invested in Port Phillip speculations led to the Depression...Two banks closed."
www.utas.edu.au

"The economy of the colonies was dependant on England and its buoyancy corresponded to harsher economic conditions in the 'mother country'. Stock and land were hard to sell due to a drought that had started in 1839. Sheep that once provided fine wool for export to England were being boiled down for tallow to make candles and soap. Speculators who bought land expecting its value to rise found that they were no longer able to sell or repay their mortgages to the bank."
http://myplace.edu.au/decades_timeline/1840/decade_landing_16_1.html?
tabRank=2&subTabRank=3

New Norfolk, November, 1839

The news from England about the falling price of wool put an arrow of terror through my heart. My sheep were worthless, the farm was drying up in front of me, with the worst drought since Van Diemen's Land was colonised, and the banks, themselves on the brink of closure, demanded their money. Closing the bedroom door, I sat cross-legged on the floor at the foot of the bed. I put my head back, closed my eyes and tried to get my mind to work through the chaos in my brain, the chaos that wouldn't let me think straight, to plan a solution.

My younger brother John, and his wife Elizabeth and their three babies left for Port Phillip months ago. Apart from my own wife and children, I have no family left in New Norfolk. Mother died in 1834, Father six months later in 1835. My older brother, James, deserted his pregnant wife and left for South Australia in January.

My neck aches from being in the same position for too long, When I am anxious my breaths are short and shallow, and that's what is happening now. It's difficult to breathe. I know the signs of a painful headache coming on. I'll have to comb my hair and straighten my clothes before I go downstairs for supper.

Margaret asked me if I was alright but didn't' wait for an answer. Her attention was diverted by eighteen-month-old Caroline putting her hands in her bowl of potato and throwing fistfuls at her sister, Maggie. The three-year-old's screams made my head pound.

I didn't want to answer Margaret. I didn't want to lie, and did I want to tell the truth. The distraction of the battle between our middle and youngest daughters gave me the opportunity to ignore my wife.

The cook, Susan, took Maggie to clean the potato off her face and clothes. While she was walking past Caroline, Maggie pulled a lump of potato out of her hair and wiped it on Caroline's face. The eighteen-month-old screamed louder than her mother did when giving birth to her.

I had to leave the table, to leave my wife, and the cook and housekeeper to sort out the battle. I wasn't hungry. Sitting on my chair on the back verandah of my two storey, three-bedroom home that also boasted a dining room and parlour, I lit my pipe and leant back in the chair. For a short, precious moment I forgot the horrors that threatened to escalate the throb at the back of my head.

Looking over the paddocks I realised they were all the colour of wheat husks. The fresh green that layered Van Diemen's Land every year since my brothers and I arrived with Mama in 1814 hadn't been seen for over a year. The merino sheep were dying of hunger, but that made no difference because the wool price in London had dropped so low they weren't worth shearing. I knew I would have to get the farm hands to organise the slaughter of the last of the cattle, so we could dry the beef. The cattle were more valuable dead, with their meat dried, than having them eat what little feed I had left. The water from the tanks kept the fruit orchard and vegetable gardens alive. We wouldn't starve.

I pulled the letter out of my pocket, the one from the bank, and read it again. It told me to pay the arrears immediately, or they'd take the farm. The irony of a bank demanding money when they were in financial trouble too, didn't make me feel any better. I screwed the letter into a ball so that it was no bigger than an egg and put it in my trouser pocket. The pang of the neck pain worked its way up both sides of my head.

Ignoring the sounds from the dining room and kitchen where Margaret, the cook, and housekeeper were grappling with our three daughters, I tiptoed upstairs. Perhaps if I went to bed my head would stop pounding.

As much as I tried to overcome the urge to work through my repetitive behaviours, nothing helped. I must perform the steps in the same order, otherwise I can't go to bed. On this night, I needed to go to bed. The pain in my head was getting worse. First, I took off my clothes and lay them on the chair in the corner of the room in the order they'd be put on in the morning. Then I washed my face and hands, this evening in cold water, because I hadn't told the housekeeper I was going to bed early. I cleaned my teeth with a rag dipped in salt. The housekeeper had put fresh salt in the bowl, along with a clean rag. I put on my nightshirt and slunk underneath the bed covers, struggling to get the garment below my knees. I had to have it below my knees and uncrumpled before I could relax. Lying on my back, looking at the ceiling, I took deep breaths as advised by the doctor to try to relieve the thumping that had travelled behind my eyes.

Closing my eyes, I let exhaustion, both physical and mental carry me to sleep.

2

MARGARET BLAY (NEE TEDDER)

She looked at the plate he'd left on the table, muttering that they could ill afford to waste food. Sitting down to finish her supper with Sarah Susanna, now five years old and aware of her father's odd behaviours, Margaret separated Maggie and Caroline. If any food was thrown, it would fall to the table or floor. Caroline refused to open her mouth when Margaret held up a spoonful for her to take. The child clamped her mouth shut, shook her head and pushed the spoon away. Not in the mood for tantrums, and angry that this was more food wasted, she called to the cook.

'Susan, please put my supper near the fire to keep warm. I'm taking Caroline to bed. If she refuses to eat, she can go to bed early, and hungry.'

Susan had been assigned to her mother, Catherine, when Margaret and her sister, Sadie lived in the house William and his younger brother John, had built on her step-father's eighty acres. Her father-in-law arranged for the convict workers. When her mother moved back to Hobart Town, with her new infant daughter, Susanna, the cook and housekeeper were reassigned to William. Susan asked Margaret if she needed help with Maggie and Sarah while she put Caroline to bed. Appreciating Susan's thoughtfulness, Margaret instructed the girls to finish their supper, while she struggled up the stairs with a screaming, thrashing, eighteen-month-old.

The door to the bedroom she shared with William was closed. She struggled past it with Caroline, the volume of the child's screams increased the closer she got to her own bedroom. Margaret dragged the child into the room and threw her on Maggie's bed to change her into her nightdress. Wrangling with the child until she was ready for bed, Margaret put her in the crib and left the room, closing the door behind her. She stood with her back against the wall, taking in deep breaths, listening to the child crying and sobbing. By the time Caroline had cried herself to sleep, Sarah and Maggie were coming up the stairs to get ready for bed. Margaret smiled at the girls. Putting her right index finger over her mouth to indicate they should be quiet, she took a little hand in each of hers and took them back downstairs into the parlour.

'You can stay up a bit longer while Mama finishes her supper. Caroline has just gone to sleep, we don't want to wake her.' Margaret explained.

'Where is Papa?' the eldest, Sarah asked.

'He went to bed early,' Margaret answered. 'He had a busy day. He was tired.'

'Why didn't he eat his supper?' Maggie wanted to know.

'I don't know,' she said, raising her voice at the girls. 'Let me eat my supper, then we'll go back upstairs.'

The three children finally tucked up in bed for the night, Margaret went into the kitchen to share a cup of tea with Susan. The cook had watched Margaret grow up, and the pair had developed a strong bond. Margaret, who could read and write, thanks to the tenacity of her mother, Catherine, encouraged Susan to apply for a Ticket of Leave. Its success meant Susan could work elsewhere, but she stayed with Margaret and William.

'I don't know what is wrong with the girls of late, Susan. They are behaving badly.'

Susan put her teacup down and reached across the table for Margaret's hands. Clasping hers around Margaret's she said, 'I think

6

their Papa's preoccupation with the state of the farm is upsetting them.'

Margaret nodded in agreement.

Going to bed after her husband meant she didn't have to witness his regimented bedtime ritual. Margaret undressed quietly, slipped on her nightshirt and slid into bed next to William who appeared to be sleeping, but restless. His legs twitched, and she could hear his teeth grinding. Even in slumber he had a frown on his forehead. She wondered what torments his dreams were delivering.

Caroline screaming about a devil, woke Margaret with a fright. She sat up straight in bed, then scrambled to get out before the child woke the whole house. In the darkness, she didn't notice William had already risen and dressed. Reaching for a candle, she lit it from the embers in the fireplace in their bedroom, wrapped a blanket around her shoulders and hurried to the girls' room. Standing up in her crib, holding onto the sides, the youngest child's screams and sobs still hadn't woken Sarah and Maggie. Margaret picked up Caroline, wrapped her in a cover from the crib, and holding the child on her left hip and the candle in her right hand, went downstairs.

William was sitting at the kitchen table finishing a cup of milk. The two nanny goats he'd seconded from his late father's farm when they were kids, ensured the children had the nourishment of the milk to drink. He used a neighbour's billy goat when nature deemed it necessary. The kids these two nanny goats bore last season, were growing, and Margaret speculated what William had intended for them.

'You are up early,' Margaret commented to her husband.

'I couldn't sleep so thought I would get an early start on the farm today. Caroline is still crying, I see.'

Margaret sat down, moving the child from her hip to her lap, and pushed the candle she had been carrying to the centre of the table. Sobs had replaced the screams, but tears still ran down Caroline's cheeks. She held the child to her, patted her back and told her everything would be all right.

William left his cup on the table, wiped his face with a clean cloth from the supply the cook left by the fire, pecked Margaret on the fore-head, and went outside into the predawn light.

Too early to get started on any activities, and still trying to keep Caroline settled, Margaret carried the child over to one of the rocking chairs placed either side of the hearth. She sat the little girl on the chair while she got the fire going. Satisfied the fire would take and burn without help for some time, she picked up Caroline, and sat in the chair with her on her lap. Rocking the chair to calm herself and her daughter, Margaret sat back, stared into the flames and wondered what was to happen to the farm.

3
___

CATHERINE

South Australian Register 14 December 1839. (www.trove.nla.gov.au)
Commercial Intelligence
Port Adelaide Shipping
Arrived
Dec 7 – The ship *Recovery* which sailed from the Port on the 6th,
brought up in Holdfast Bay to take in stock for Port Lincoln.
8 – The brig *Porter*, 230 tons, W. Murray commander, from Hobart
Town, 24th November, with a cargo of sundries. Passengers – Mr and
Mrs Bowman, Mrs Blay.

Hobart Town, November 1839

Carrying her five-month-old infant, Susanna, Catherine watched as the driver loaded her belongings into the back of the wagon. It wasn't a long way from her home in Murray Street to the Hobart waterfront, but too far to carry a baby and push her belongings along. She had the money from the sale of her first husband's flour mill, and the sale of the house he bought for them when his seven-year sentence ended. With one last glance at the home, she thought she saw Teddy standing in the doorway, waving to her. Closing her eyes tight and opening them again, he'd disappeared.

Her husband, James Blay Jr, went to South Australia in January leaving her, three months with child, to live with her two married daughters. When told about the expected baby, he'd denied parentage and absconded. In September he wrote to Catherine and asked her to bring Susanna and join him in Adelaide. The tone of his letter brought joy to her heart. He said he missed her, wanted to see his daughter and had started a successful shoemaking business in the new Colony. Catherine hadn't told her adult daughters, Margaret and Sadie that she was going to South Australia to join her husband. She would ask him write to them when she arrived. She visited the solicitor in Hobart to ask for a letter to be sent to James, telling him she and Susanna would be on the brig *Porter*, arriving in Port Adelaide around the 8th December.

At the invitation of the driver, Catherine took the offer of help to get onto the wagon, baby Susanna handed to her when she was seated. She didn't look over her shoulder at the house she would never live in again; she stared straight ahead, deciding it was better to look forward to her new life, not behind. Apart from her two married daughters, there was no reason to stay in Van Diemen's Land. Her youngest sister, Betsy was going to Port Phillip, her older sister, Sophia died in 1835, her mother died in 1836, her mother-in-law died in 1834, and her father-in-law in 1835. She needed her husband by her side.

James waved from the dock. Catherine, excited, waved back, then hurried down to her quarters to tidy her appearance. She combed her hair, stuffed it under her cap, tied the cap under her chin, and straightened her dress. She put a new hat on Susanna to keep the sun off, as much as to hide her almost bald head: the infant's hair was so fair, it couldn't be seen. She picked up her travelling bag, leaving the larger bags for collection by the porter, and went back on deck.

James stood, waiting.

Catherine's heart skipped a beat when she saw her husband. She ached for his touch, to feel his arms around her, his lips on hers. Almost dropping Susanna while her mind wandered she secured the child on her right hip, slung her travel bag over her left shoulder, and made her way across the gangplank to the waiting arms of her husband.

Susanna squirmed and struggled while her parents embraced. James kissed Catherine with such passion, she thought he wouldn't be able to wait until they were in the house. He fondled her breasts and pushed himself against her. She felt his manhood rise in anticipation and pushed him away.

'James, take a breath. I am as anxious as you, but there are things that need our attention.'

He stepped back, nodded and looked at the five-month-old baby girl staring at him. The infant smiled, James grinned.

Catherine let a wave of relief wash over her.

The house was a few doors away from his shoemaking business. Catherine hoped they would be happier here than in New Norfolk in the house behind James Sr's shop. They'd lived there, paying James Sr rent, while her husband set up a farm on his eighty acres. She had been miserable, her husband moody, belligerent and difficult. Here, in Adelaide, fourteen years later, he looked happy.

James showed Catherine into the house. The double bed hadn't been made for some time, and there didn't appear to be anywhere for baby Susanna to sleep. A modest kitchen presented a tiny fireplace, a sideboard, a large metal tub and a small wooden table with two chairs. Catherine's head tingled with anxiety. She didn't want to let James know how disappointed she felt and didn't want to upset him.

'It's lovely, James. We will be happy here.'

He grabbed her by the shoulders, pulled her toward him and kissed her hungrily. Susanna, still being held by her mother, screamed with fright.

'Put her down somewhere so we can get to know each other again.' James ordered.

Catherine looked around for somewhere clean to set the baby down, the tingling in the back of her head increased.

'There doesn't seem to be anywhere suitable, James. Do you have a crib for her?'

He huffed, marched toward the bed, grabbed a pillow and put it on the floor at the foot of the bed. 'Put her here.'

Catherine took off Susanna's hat and lay her on the pillow. The infant was indignant at being put down. Clenching her fists, she waved her arms in the air, kicked her legs, closed her eyes and cried louder than the foghorns on the boats in the harbour.

James pulled Catherine to him and put his hands under her dress. He fumbled through her petticoat until he found what he was looking for. Her feet moved apart to give him easier access. He grunted as he fingered her and kissed her with hunger more than desire. Leading her to the bed while Susanna cried on the pillow on the floor, James pushed her clothing up over her head, and with brute force, penetrated her. She gasped in pain, glad he couldn't see her face It was over in an instant. At least in the bedroom, he hadn't changed.

Susanna's cries intensified.

'Make her stop,' he said as he pulled up his trousers. 'I'll see if I can find something to use as a crib. There's bound to be something, somewhere.' He left the house.

Catherine struggled to put her feet on the floor, in pain from his rough treatment. Picking up Susanna she crawled back onto the bed, put the pillow behind her and fed her baby.

'Oh, Susanna, what have I done?' she murmured to the suckling infant.

4

BETSY

"... Thus on the Tuesday and Wednesday, October 29 and 30, the new arrivals were all "landed in the ship's boats at the beach opposite Williamstown, and having walked overland two miles to the banks of the Yarra Yarra..."

From:
https://poi-australia.com.au/melbourne-in-the-1840s

New Norfolk December 1839

What do you mean, she's gone back to him? She's gone to South Australia? I don't believe it.'

On a trip to Hobart Town, John Lilley Pearce, Betsy's husband called on Catherine to find she had sold the flour mill and sailed to South Australia.

'I'm sorry, my love, but this is the case. She took the infant, she left Hobart on 24 November.' John explained to his wife.

'How do you know?' Betsy demanded.

'They print the ships' sailing dates and cargo and passengers in the newspaper. When I discovered someone else living in the house, I asked at the Post Office [1] They had newspapers, I looked.'

Since her marriage to James Blay Jr in 1823, Betsy's older sister, Catherine, had been abandoned by her husband and reunited with him so often they'd lost count.

'Well, at least now we can continue packing for our move to Port Phillip and I won't have to worry about being another person who abandons my sister.'

Wiping her eyes with her apron, Betsy walked into the bedroom and closed the door. She sat on the edge of the bed and let the tears run from her eyes. Her sister not only returned to that fiend of a man but didn't even bother to tell her. She wondered if Margaret and Sadie knew.

Not being able to read or write had been a burden for Betsy, a burden she blamed her parents for. Although her father was literate, he didn't think it was important for his daughters to be educated, even a little. Betsy would have to ask John or her eldest son, James, to write a letter for her for delivery to Catherine's daughters, Margaret and Sadie.

It was a blessing that Catherine had run back to James. Since she and John had decided to move to Port Phillip, Betsy had struggled with the idea of leaving her sister in Van Diemen's Land. Her niece, Margaret had confided in her that William was agitating to move to Port Phillip too. Both women felt the angst of leaving Catherine in Van Diemen's Land. Sadie was in New Norfolk, settled and happy with Felix but if they decided to move, Catherine would be completely alone. Betsy slapped her hands together and gave them a shake. The problem of deserting her sister no longer a concern.

With the farm sold, the convicts were returned to the Assignment Board.[2] Betsy hoped the cook and housekeeper would find a suitable situation. She knew some settlers treated assigned convicts poorly; the women had served her family well and deserved appropriate respect.

John Pearce and his sons, James 19 and William, 17, packed up the farm. New owners bought the property at a reduced price. The drop in the value of wool in London, and the drought created havoc and John wanted to leave and start again in a new colony, and Betsy looked for an escape from the convict connections that tied them and the children to Van Diemen's Land.

The Pearce family loaded their bags onto the steamship on the Derwent and travelled to Hobart to board a schooner, bound for Port Phillip. Betsy watched as John's face lit up with excitement. She knew he loved the sea and was looking forward to the voyage across Bass Strait.

In December 1839, after two days at sea, the Pearce family arrived in Port Phillip. Betsy stood on the deck of the schooner, put her hand up to shade her eyes from the sun and looked to her husband for reassurance.

'There's nothing, here,' she said to John. 'Where are the streets and the buildings and the...there's no organisation.' Her shoulders slumped. Putting one arm around her daughter, Louisa, and holding her travel bag in the other hand, Betsy froze to the spot.

'This is Williamstown, Betsy, Melbourne is two miles away. We have to walk there.'

John unwound Betsy's fingers from the handle of her bag, put his hand in hers, and lead her toward the ladder to climb down into the small boat for the short trip to land.

'Hobart Town was worse than this when I arrived there, Betsy. And now it is a real town, with real streets, buildings and houses. We are pioneers.' He grinned. 'Don't you remember what Hobart Town was like when you arrived there in January 1808 with your parents and sisters? And New Norfolk, that wasn't even surveyed, I believe.'

'I was three years' old, John,' Betsy remonstrated, 'I don't remember.'

Pleased she had worn her working shoes and not her slippers, Betsy refused the support offered by her eldest son, and climbed out of the small boat, determined to be independent. Lifting her dress out of the water, she waded to the beach, leaving John to carry his and her bag. Louisa's brothers helped her from the boat, to the beach.

Not showing any signs of fatigue, John grinned at his wife, patted his sons on the back, and hugged Louisa into his side. 'We will do well. We can leave the poor wool prices, the drought, and the convict past behind. I'll get a job while we plan our future.'

Joining the other passengers from the schooner, the Pearce family picked up their belongings. James and William carried the heavier bags and set a comfortable walking pace to Melbourne.

Standing in Collins Street, Betsy put down her travelling bag, took off her cap, flattened her hair with her hands, pulled some unruly strands into place, and placed the cap back on her head. She smoothed down her dress, and rubbed one foot over the other, trying to clean the dust off her shoes. Glaring at John she asked where they were going next. 'As I said in Williamstown, there is nothing here,' she snarled.

3

5
_____

SARAH (SADIE) AND FELIX

New Norfolk, December 1839

R ead it again, please, Felix. I want to think on every word.'
Sadie's husband, Felix McCabe Murray, sat opposite her on
his favourite chair on the back verandah. The airless summer heat
made each breath an effort. He took off his hat, wiped his face and
forehead with a handkerchief he kept in his trouser pocket, hooked
his hat on the back of his chair, cleared his throat, and read the letter
again to his wife.

December 1839

My dearest Margaret and Sadie.

*Your cousin, James, is writing this letter for me, as I dictate to him. I
have to report to you that on a visit to your mother, and my sister,
Catherine, in Hobart Town recently, my husband John, discovered
she no longer lived in Murray Street. Making enquiries at the Post
Office, he learned that she sailed for Adelaide, South Australia,*

arriving there on 24 November. She, of course, had your half-sister Susanna, with her. I have not heard a word from her.

This can only mean she has returned to James Blay Jr. I leave Van Diemen's Land knowing I have done all I can to support my sister. My family and I will begin a new life in Port Phillip.

Our love to you and your families.

Aunt Betsy

Sadie wiped her daughter, Margaret's face as she finished eating a pear. Staring over the vegetable garden she and the assigned convict housekeeper had planted, she said 'We must harvest the onions and pickle them.'

Felix moved from his chair to his wife. Kneeling in front of her, he picked up her hands and clasped them in his. 'There is nothing you can do about your mother, Sadie. She will always go back to him.'

'Oh, Felix. Why does she do it? What will become of Susanna?' Sadie stood and let her husband hold her while she cried the tears of those lies that her mother had believed for sixteen years.

The journey to her sister Margaret's farm, Stoney Bank, didn't take long in the buggy. Felix encouraged the pony to move along by a click, clicking of his tongue, and holding the reins, moving his arms up and down so they tapped the animal's back. He didn't believe in causing any creature harm. Sadie didn't feel that way about her step-father. She would happily push him under the feet of the trotting pony, but it would annoy Felix because it would startle the animal. No, better to take the whip that Felix never used...Sadie shook her head to rid it of the nonsense. She would never see James Blay Jr again, no point imagining how she could get revenge for the years of suffering he caused her mother.

'Sadie, Felix, thank you for coming.' Margaret kissed her sister on the cheek and pecked her brother-in-law on his flushed, overheated, Irish face. 'William is in Hobart Town on business. We'll sit in the back under that big gum tree.'

The cook brought lemonade to drink and sliced pears and apples to eat, placing them on a small table under the tree. Felix stacked three chairs from the kitchen and carried them outside. His pale Irish skin pulsed red; it reminded Sadie of the time the bees stung her.

'Do you remember when you annoyed the bees, Sadie, and they attacked you?' Margaret asked.

'Yes. What made you remember that?'

'Felix's red face reminded me of yours that day, all those stings stuck in your face, arms and hands. I thought you would die.'

'I think Mama did, too. Just as well Papa...' Sadie stopped mid-sentence, got up from her seat and leaned against the big gum tree. Biting her lip to stop the tears, she looked at her sister. 'What are we to do about Mama?'

'William says there is nothing we can do.'

'As do I,' interjected Felix. 'Your mother will keep going back to him. She is a grown woman with a mind of her own.'

'That time he saved me from those bees and removed all the stings and helped me recover. Times like those we saw in him what Mama must have. But he is bad more than he is good.' Sighing in resignation, Sadie returned to the seat under the tree. 'I have concerns that our half-sister, Susanna, will grow up like her father.'

6

BETSY

Melbourne, District of Port Phillip, 1840

The boys found employment within three days of their arrival in Melbourne and their father joined them on the same work site two days' later. They worked on a wooden church, in the bush, to the north of the town. [1] Melbourne was expanding, it had a vitality to it that Betsy had not remembered in Hobart Town or New Norfolk.

John secured the family accommodation in one of the thirteen hotels, this one in Collins Street, and he and his sons left each morning, making their way through the dirt streets, to work.

They occupied three rooms in the hotel and ate in the dining room with the other guests. Eager to save money to fund their new start, Betsy negotiated a reduced rent for her services as a cook, and Louisa's as a housemaid. With every member of the family employed, Betsy allowed herself the privilege of thinking about a new future, a future where her children didn't have to explain if they were free settlers to Van Diemen's Land or born there of convict parents or grandparents. The scorn for convict connections, aggravated under Lt Governor Arthur continued to fester. Melbourne displayed no such bias. They lost the convict stain in the sea between Hobart Town and Port Phillip.

Climbing into bed next to her husband, Betsy rejected his embrace. 'I'm tired, I work all day as you do, I want to sleep.'

———

Two weeks after they arrived in Melbourne, Betsy woke to the sun bursting through the curtain less window. It shone on her face. She sat up with a start, her brain trying to work out where she was, and the time. Pushing back the covers, she swung her legs onto the floor, pulled her hair off her face and stepped quietly over to the chair in the corner of the room where her clothes waited. Each day started at dawn, long before the guests in the hotel surfaced. She sat on the small stool in front of the dresser, forced her wayward hair into a bun and covered it with her cap. John was stirring, he would be up soon.

The same shards of sunlight that penetrated her dreams a few minutes ago, lit the stairs. An east-facing window the only source of light, she imagined a candle or lamp would be needed in the winter months to navigate the stairs at this hour.

The coals in the hearth in the kitchen stove were glowing. Prodding the fire until it stirred to life, Betsy lifted the kettle onto its cradle to boil and added wood to the coals. Already perspiring, she wiped her forehead and organised breakfast for the guests who would be soon filtering into the dining room. Her husband and sons walked in first, James and William kissed their mother good morning, and sat at the table helping themselves to the bread, boiled eggs and goat's milk. John nodded at Betsy, poured himself a cup of tea and drank it in the kitchen. Putting two eggs in his pocket he walked into the dirt road that was Collins Street to make his way to the church at the north end of the township.

Betsy noticed her sons looking at each other. James raised both eyebrows, and William shrugged his shoulders. They got up from the table, said goodbye to their mother, collected their coats and hats from the foyer and walked outside.

Betsy cleared dishes from the tables, wondering why her daughter had not yet appeared. Walking into the kitchen laden with crockery, she frowned at Louisa who sat stirring a spoon around in her bowl of oatmeal. 'You are late, again, Louisa. Go into the dining room and clear the tables.'

Scowling, her daughter pushed the bowl away and stomped into the dining room, indifferent to the display of undisciplined behaviour.

───────

'Louisa's behaviour today was most unladylike, ungracious, and downright rude.' Betsy complained to her husband as they readied for bed. 'She argued about her duties, refused to empty the chamber pots, and left me to clean up the dining room after breakfast.'

'She doesn't want to be a housekeeper,' John answered, 'she wants to be the lady of the house, not a servant in one.'

'How do you know?' Betsy retaliated.

'She told me. She hates working in the hotel.'

Betsy crawled into bed, physically exhausted and again refused her husband's advances. 'I don't know how she thinks she will be the lady of the house in this Colony.' Betsy mumbled.

'Good morning, Mr Waldon,' Betsy greeted one of the other guests as he made his way into the dining room. William Waldon moved into the hotel two weeks after the Pearce family and worked on one of the many building sites in the new township of Melbourne. Going out of his way to speak to her every morning, Betsy realised she looked for him at the start of each day. His attention brightened her mood.

───────

'Don't push me away tonight,' John scolded his wife. 'You haven't lain with me for months. A man needs a release. I don't care how tired you are. I too am tired. I walk to work, work like a slave all day, walk back, eat, go to bed, and you can't even give me a moment's pleasure.'

Betsy submitted to her husband's demands, promising herself this would be the last time. She wanted a new life, a genuine new start in this new Colony, and William Waldon had promised it to her.

She didn't expect Louisa's ultimatum, nor her son, William's, dismissal of her promise to always love her children. Her eldest, James, was the only one to stand by her. Her middle child and her daughter sided with their father in the matrimonial breakup and opted to return to Van Diemen's Land with him.

Betsy choked back tears while John helped Louisa into the wagon, and William stowed their bags.

'Goodbye, Mother,' William said with such venom Betsy could feel the roots of her hair tingle.

'You know where we'll be,' Louisa scoffed. 'Goodbye, James. I hope you are happy staying here with her.'

Betsy and her eldest child stepped back to avoid the cloud of dust the wagon stirred up as it moved away. James put his arm around her shoulders and led her into the kitchen of the hotel.

'We had better sit down and make plans,' said William Waldon, a huge grin plastered over his grimy, brown face.

7

WILLIAM

New Norfolk, 1840

I sat in the waiting area of the auctioneer's office. Beads of perspiration formed on my forehead and ran into my eyes. Using the back of my hand to wipe them away, made my hand sweaty. The handkerchief hidden in my pocket cleaned my hands, but more perspiration formed on my brow. I don't know how many times I repeated the process of wiping and cleaning until the auctioneer, Mr John Stracey, asked me into his office.

He offered me a seat on the other side of the desk and began with small talk. I was eager for an opinion, so pressed him about the value of my property.

'If you were to sell the property at this time,' he said, 'I value it between £1800 and £2000.'

That was a good price considering the economic downturn, and I wanted to get out of his office as soon as I could, to work through an economic solution. I stood, leaned over the desk, shook Mr Stracey's hand and took my leave. Different scenarios played in my head while walking back to the farm. None of them included staying in New Norfolk. I owed money to several people in New Norfolk and Hobart

Town. If I could sell the land at a good price I could repay my debts and fund a move for the family to Port Phillip. But I also entertained the idea of selling the farm for less than Mr Stracey's valuation, keeping all the funds and moving to Port Phillip before any debtors realised I'd left. By the time I walked from the auctioneer's office in New Norfolk to the farm, I'd made my decision.

I took off my boots and placed them under the seat in the boot room at the back of the house. My hat went on a hook, the same hook I used each time I entered the house. My jacket hung on a hook directly under the hat. Then I lined my boots up with the jacket and hat. Only after everything was in its place, did I walk into the noisy kitchen.

The cook was kneading dough for bread, each time she threw the ball of dough on the table, my head pounded. Sarah Susanna practised her writing, calling out each letter as she wrote it. Her fingers, covered with ink, looked as if they were gangrenous and about to fall off. It annoyed me that she wasted the expensive ink. Balancing Caroline on her hip, Margaret consoled three-year-old Maggie who was screaming about something I couldn't decipher. I stood in my stockinged feet, looking from my wife and children and back.

'There is a lot of noise in this house.' I said, raising my voice.

All but Maggie stopped what they were doing and looked at me. Maggie kept screaming for her mother.

'I am going into the parlour to think. You will all be quiet.'

Stepping aside to let me walk through to the parlour, Margaret asked me what was wrong.

'We will talk later. When the children are in bed and it is quiet.'

Thinking I should acknowledge the children, I patted Sarah on the head and smiled at Caroline, shutting the kitchen door behind me.

I lay on the chaise lounge with my head on the armrest, hoping it would relieve the nagging pain in my neck. I listened to the children moving between laughing and crying, wondering how Margaret kept up with all their demands. I'd decided how the future would look for my family, so I closed my eyes, and tried to rest.

'William, supper is ready.'

Margaret coaxed me from sleep, patting my arm and moving her hand over my forehead. It reminded me of my mother when we were on the *HMS Kangaroo* on the way to New South Wales.

'Are you well? You look pale.'

I felt more relaxed than I had for some months. 'I am fine, my dear. Let's have supper. I'll tell you about my plans when the children are in bed.'

My night-time ritual completed, I pulled back the bedclothes, and slid underneath, next to my wife. The sight of her, her hair splayed across the pillow, her face clean and pink, her nightdress unlaced enough to reveal her ample bosom, had my manhood react with no other encouragement. I pulled Margaret to me, made sure she was ready to receive my rigid, pulsing manhood and penetrated her with more vigour than I had roused for weeks.

We lay on our backs, me panting and Margaret pulling down her nightdress, when she asked what I wanted to talk about.

'I am selling the farm and we are moving to Port Phillip. I want to go before the end of the year.'

I think Margaret had expected this announcement since my younger brother John, and her own Aunt Betsy had moved to the new Colony. And now her mother had run to South Australia after my no-good older brother, it left her sister Sadie, and my friend Felix Murray, as the only family left in Van Diemen's Land.

'You mustn't do anything yet, or tell anyone,' I told her, feeling my voice quavering and my face reddening. 'I have matters to attend to before we make it known. Say nothing to the convicts.'

I pulled the nightshirt below my knees, turned away from Margaret, pulled the covers up to just below my ear, and fell into a sleep that for the first time in months, didn't fill the darkness with fear.

8

CATHERINE

Adelaide, South Australia, July 1840.

Catherinr celebrated Susanna's first birthday alone. She had made no friends in the new Colony; all her time was spent creating a thriving vegetable garden and trying to turn the shack she and James lived in into a home. And caring for Susanna. He'd brought home a packing crate when she and the baby arrived, telling Catherine to use it as a crib for Susanna. The infant had outgrown it and he wasn't interested in supplying anything more appropriate.

While Susanna slept in the middle of Catherine and James' bed, Catherine dug up potatoes, bagged them, collected eggs which she put in a cloth bag she'd made, pulled onions from the ground, and prepared her products for sale. With the front door ajar so she could hear if her child woke, Catherine took the kitchen table into the street, and set up a stall to sell her produce. Newcomers to the Colony who were establishing themselves paid well for Catherine's fresh vegetables and eggs.

As Susanna stirred, crying for her mother, Catherine sold the last of the potatoes. Dragging the kitchen table back into the house, she cleaned off any evidence of her stall, and hid the money under the pillow in the fruit crate that Susanna slept in when James was there.

Sitting the child on a blanket on the floor in the middle of the room that served as a kitchen, dining room, parlour and bedroom, Catherine told her daughter stories of New Norfolk and Hobart. She spoke of Susanna's grandparents, James and Elizabeth Cullen and James and Sarah Blay, of her Aunts Sophia and Betsy, her uncles, William and John, and her sisters, Margaret and Sadie, while she prepared the ingredients to make a cake for Susanna's first birthday. Trading with a neighbour, Catherine had exchanged onions and potatoes for goat's milk and jam to add to the cake. The little girl played with a doll Catherine had sewn for her.

Susanna crawled towards the hearth as her mother was putting the final touches to the cake mixture. The little girl tried to pull herself up using the bricks surrounding the fireplace. She slipped. Catherine dropped the cake pan as Susanna's screams curdled her blood. The child's hands were in the hot coals of the fire, her nose and mouth bled from the impact with the hearth bricks. Picking up her child, Catherine held Susanna to her, struggling to soothe her daughter and look for a salve for her hands and a cloth for her nose and mouth at the same time. She put Susanna down on the blanket, the child's cries of terror matched the dread Catherine felt. Finding the pork fat Catherine knelt on the floor next to Susanna and spread the fat over the child's hands. The little girl's cries of agony broke Catherine's heart. Remembering Sadie's life-threatening bee stings, she wished she had honey to put on Susanna's burns. Catherine lifted her dress and tore strips off her petticoat, wetting one she wiped Susanna's nose and mouth. The child winced in pain and screamed louder. Her nose looked broken. Catherine wet more pieces of her petticoat and wrapped them around her child's hands; she picked her up off the floor and sat on the bed, leaning her back against the wall. Although Susanna had recently been weaned, Catherine put her to the breast as a comfort for the little girl. Susanna closed her eyes and sobbed as she suckled, exhaustion sending her to sleep in Catherine's arms.

. . .

'We can't stay here Susanna,' Catherine said 'We are alone, we have only each other. We have to go back to Tasmania.'

'What happened to her? Why is her nose crooked and her hands swollen and red?' James didn't greet Catherine or Susanna. The moment he saw the little girl he demanded answers.

Explaining what happened, Catherine found it difficult to reconcile her husband's fury at the injuries to the child, with his ignoring her and denying his parentage.

'I thought honey might have helped her burns, like you used on Sadie when she was little, but I couldn't find any.' Catherine hoped the reference to the past and how James had saved Sadie's life would temper his mood. It had the opposite effect. He flew into a rage, banged his fists on the table and accused her of being a neglectful mother.

Susanna cried.

'Make her be quiet,' James bellowed. He slammed the door behind him as he left the shack.

Again, Catherine picked up Susanna to comfort her. James' tantrums made the little girl uneasy, and she clung to her mother, burying her head on her shoulder. Catherine held her.

Counting the money she had hidden in the makeshift crib, Catherine knew she still had more potatoes, onions and eggs to sell to raise enough funds to return to Tasmania. James had taken the money she'd brought with her from the sale of the house in Hobart, saying he would use it to develop his business. Pleased she had listened to the voice in her head that told her to leave the proceeds from the sale of the flour mill with her father-in-law's solicitor, Catherine would be able to finance a life in Tasmania.

November 1840

Catherine wasn't sure where the equal of Hobart's Wapping was in Adelaide, but she had suspicions that James frequented the brothels and the illegal drinking establishments. He had lost interest in her in the bedroom, only spoke to her when necessary, and never paid attention to Susanna. He often left the apprentice to run his shoe-making business and disappeared for days at a time.

Saving enough funds to travel home to Tasmania, Catherine dressed Susanna, put the money she'd hoarded on the toddler's head, and covered it with a hat. She tied the hat under Susanna's chin and held her hand while the toddler shambled along beside her through the dirt streets of Adelaide. If James saw them walking and approached them, the money would stay hidden.

Apart from the hotels, the shipping office was the busiest place in Adelaide. Catherine remembered the Convict Administration Office as being the busiest place in Hobart Town when she and Teddy lived there. There were no convicts in South Australia. James told her the advertising to encourage settlers said it was a free colony.

Susanna lifted her arms to be picked up, Catherine balanced her on her hip and jostled through the small crowd to get to the counter.

'When is the first boat sailing to Hobart Town?' she asked the clerk.

'The *Abeona* missus,' said the clerk. 'She leaves on the 6th at seven in the forenoon. Ya have ta be on board by six in the forenoon or she'll sail without ya.'

Being unable to read and write, Catherine was never sure of the date. 'What is today's date please, sir,' she asked.

'The fourth,' came the reply. 'She's fillin' up fast. If you want ta book a ticket, best do so straight away.'

The barriers to her being able to escape so soon, banged against each other in Catherine's mind; but knowing she couldn't bring Susanna up in the environment created by James' indifference and contempt, she removed the child's hat and pushed the money over the counter.

With her ticket hidden under Susanna's hat, Catherine encouraged the toddler to walk back to the shack. Dust covered her little shoes and as she dragged her feet, her stockings took on the colour of the dirt road.

'Where have you been?' James demanded when she opened the door. Thinking of a believable response as quickly as possible, Catherine said she'd taken Susanna for a walk in the spring sunshine, adding 'She is walking now and needs to practise.'

Her husband had a way of screwing up his face when he wasn't interested in what was being said. 'I'll just clean her up a little and then get you something to eat, James,' she told him.

'Don't bother, I'm going out. I've been waiting for over an hour, I want nothing now.' He took his hat off the peg near the door, patted it in his place on his head, and left Catherine to take breaths to relieve her anxiety and to secret away the ticket.

Not wanting to hide the ticket in her travelling bag, Catherine put it under the makeshift mattress in Susanna's crib. Taking off the toddler's dusty shoes and stockings, Catherine whispered her plans to the little girl. 'We will leave tomorrow, Susanna. I have enough money, we'll stay in the boarding house near the wharf, so we get on the ship in time. As soon as your Papa leaves in the morning, I'll pack, and we'll go.'

If he came back before the ship sailed, he might look for her. Dread crawled down her back. As his wife, she would have to obey him and return to the shack. 'I don't think he will look for us, Susanna. He has all the money I brought with me.'

James Blay Jr left the shack before sunrise on the morning of the 5th November 1840. He didn't speak to his wife or acknowledge his daughter.

Catherine lay in bed until she heard the rooster crow. Susanna slept. Creeping around the timbers on the floor that had been laid directly on the ground, with no foundations, Catherine dressed. She put on the two petticoats she owned, the two dresses, one over the other, two pairs of stockings and her jacket. The more she wore, the less she had to carry to the boarding house. She'd pack properly once there. Susanna's clothes were easier to stow. She put the child's doll on top of the clothes in the bag, picked up her daughter out of the crib, wrapped a blanket around her, including covering her head, reached under the mattress for the ticket which she then stuffed down her bodice, balanced both bags over her free shoulder, and without thinking about one last look around, scurried out into the street.

Complaining about being woken, Susanna wriggled in her mother's arms. 'Stop it, Susanna. Keep still, we don't have far to go.' As if sensing her mother's anxiety, Susanna quietened while Catherine struggled up the street toward the boarding house.

The *Abeona* stood at anchor just past the wharf.

Catherine glanced over her shoulder to see if her husband had caught her out and decided to follow.

James Blay didn't look for his wife and daughter.

Nov 21 - The schooner, <u>Abeona</u>, 96 tons, Blackburn from Port Adelaide, 6th instant, in ballast, J.F. Strachan, agent...Mrs Blay...[1]

Hobart Town, November 1840

Too embarrassed to contact her older daughters just yet, Catherine first visited the office of the solicitor who had charge of the funds from the sale of James Tedder's flour mill.

On giving her the money, the solicitor advised her to buy a house to take advantage of Hobart's growth. 'You will always have something to sell if you need money in the future, Mrs Blay.'

Catherine put the money in her bag, balanced Susanna on her hip and walked back to the boarding house, careful to avoid the cottage in Murray Street Tedder had bought all those years ago. In her room, Catherine put her daughter down to play, leaned back on the bed with her hands under her head, and smiled. She would never go back to James Blay Jr. He was finally out of her system. She and Susanna would be happier without him.

9
___

WILLIAM AND MARGARET

"In the matter of the insolvency of William Blay, late of New Norfolk,
in Van Diemen's Land, Farmer.
To the creditors of the above-named William Blay, and also to the
said William Blay himself, or his agent, if he be absent from the
Colony.
NOTICE IS HEREBY GIVEN, that R? Joseph, of New Norfolk,
Storekeeper, a creditor of the said William Blay, did on the sixth day
of March instant, present a petition to William Sorell, Esquire,
Commissioner of Insolvent Estates for Hobart Town, setting forth the
matters and things required by the Act of Council instituted 'An Act
for the more effectual distribution of Insolvent Estates' and praying
that he the said William Blay might be declared insolvent, and that
his Estates and Effects might be distributed generally amongst his
creditors and the said petition having been heard before the said
Commissioner on the said ninth day of March, instant, he the said
Commissioner did declare the said William Blay, Insolvent, within
the meaning of the before-mentioned Act of Council, and appointed
Andrew Crombie, of Hobart Town, aforesaid, Esquire, Provincial
Assignee, of the Estate and Effects of the said Insolvent, and further
appointed Wednesday, the thirty-first day of March instant, at ten

o'clock in the forenoon, at the Court House, Hobart Town, aforesaid, for the first meeting of the Creditors of the said Insolvent, and for the otherwise proceeding in the matter of such insolvency.

Dated this ninth day of March 1841,
J. Blizard Stanley
Solicitor to the said Insolvency."[1]

New Norfolk January 1841

Sadie and Felix stood on the banks of the Derwent while William secured his pregnant wife and his three daughters onto the steamer. Felix helped William stow the bags. Sadie's efforts at stopping the tears from running down her cheeks, failed.

Margaret straightened her hat and blew a kiss towards her sister and niece and brother-in-law. 'I love you, Sadie,' she called as the steamer pulled away from the jetty. 'I'll write when we are settled.'

Sadie and her husband, Felix McCabe Murray, waved until the boat was out of sight. Putting his arms around his distraught wife, Felix helped her up the embankment and into the wagon.

'You still haven't told me why we had to leave in such a hurry, William,' Margaret said to her husband. 'We have left all our furniture, two horses, a dairy cow, the sow with a litter of five, the cattle and a calf, twenty ducks, two tons of hay, and all the farming implements. [2] Who will look after it all?'

'I sold it to Mr Turnbull. It is up to him what he does with the farm and the furniture.'

'But why did we leave in such a hurry? Not even a chance to say goodbye to my cousins.'

William wrung his hands together then wiped them on his trousers, then took off his hat and ran his fingers through his hair.

Margaret waited. She stared, hoping the pressure of her look would bring forth an explanation.

'I am declared insolvent.' He let the words settle. He watched the colour drain from Margaret's face, he watched as she dry-retched, trying to keep calm in front of the children. 'I sold the farm for much less than it is worth, so I could secure the funds for our escape to Port Phillip. We'll start again. The recession in Van Diemen's Land ruined me.'

Margaret stared at the dirty floor of the steamer as it chuffed up the Derwent. She took deep breaths to stop herself from vomiting and from screaming obscenities at her husband.

Watching New Norfolk disappear, William felt a chasm of sadness develop in his heart. Apart from London, this was the only home he knew, and London was the memory of a five-year-old boy, not of the father and husband he saw in the mirror each day. Margaret had lived nowhere else. His parents were buried in New Norfolk, her father in Hobart. The house her grandfather built even though sold, stood sentry overlooking the Derwent.

Watching his three daughters brought a flicker of hope. They would have the opportunities of a new colony free from the convict heritage that followed him and Margaret. That's what he told himself. It made leaving their home a little easier. He hadn't failed; the economy had failed him. If the court had just given him more time, he would have been able to sell the farm, the equipment, the livestock, clear his debts and make a new start without having to skulk around in fear of being caught.

The steamboat made travel to Hobart Town quicker, but restlessness still took hold of the children. Margaret was at least five months into her fourth pregnancy and fatigue slunk around her body for most of the day, every day. Two-year-old Caroline's behaviour, hard to manage on land, was impossible on the small steamboat. The eldest, six-year-old Sarah followed Caroline around, ensuring she didn't fall overboard. William stared at the banks of the Derwent ignorant of the strain placed on his wife.

'Where are we going, Mama?' Sarah asked. 'Why was Aunt Sadie crying?'

Picking up Caroline and sitting her on her knee, and making Maggie sit next to her on the bench seat, Margaret struggled to answer her daughter. She glanced at William. He looked away. 'We are going to a new place to live. We'll be sailing over the seas. It will be a big adventure.'

His eyes bulging, head shaking, William mouthed to Margaret to be quiet. The riskiest part of their journey would be moving from the steamboat to the brig *Lord Hobart* for the trip to Port Phillip. If creditors approached the children and asked questions while William was securing the family's passage, he would be gaoled.

Margaret rubbed her belly and murmured that she hoped this child would also be a girl. She wasn't amenable to William getting his wish for a son - not this time.

'Grandmama is over there,' Sarah squealed with excitement as the steamboat was manoeuvred to the dock. 'We can say goodbye to her and Susanna.'

Catherine waved to her daughter and granddaughters; Susanna copied. The solicitor had written to Margaret and Sadie to say Catherine was back in Hobart.

Hugging her mother and bending down to kiss her half-sister, Margaret asked if she and the girls could freshen up in Catherine's room at the boarding house. She walked to William who was helping the steamboat captain unload their bags. 'The girls and I are going to Mama's room to freshen up. Caroline needs a sleep. You will find us there when you are ready.' Without waiting for a response, Margaret turned, grabbed Caroline's hand, told Sarah to take Maggie's hand, and followed her mother to the boarding house.

Margaret took off Caroline's shoes and lay her on the bed. The child was grumpy and grizzling. 'Maggie, lay down next to your sister, see if she will have a sleep with you there.'

Catherine's room didn't have a lot of furniture, but it looked comfortable and clean. Margaret sat in one of the armchairs by the window, her mother sat in the other. Sarah entertained Susanna on the floor.

'How long will you stay here, Mama?' Margaret asked.

'I don't know.' I will have to find work to support us. I'll speak to Sadie and Felix. If I can find a small cottage in New Norfolk Sadie might help with Susanna when I work.' She smiled at her youngest daughter as she played on the floor.

'Did you know Uncle John and William and Louisa have come back from Port Phillip?' Margaret asked her mother.

Catherine lurched forward in the armchair. 'What are you saying?'

'Uncle John has left Aunt Betsy. William and Louisa came back with him. Aunt Betsy is with someone else, his name is William something or other. James stayed with her.'

Catherine stood and paced the room, stepping over the girls playing on the floor. 'Why would Betsy stay with someone else?' she asked, 'John is a good man.'

'Louisa didn't like it in Port Phillip. Apparently Aunt Betsy had her working as a housemaid to get money off their rent in the hotel. When Uncle John caught Aunt Betsy with the other man, Louisa was glad to get out of the work she hated,' Margaret explained.

'Will you look for Aunt Betsy when you get to Port Phillip, Margaret? Will you write to me at Sadie's letting me know how she is?'

Margaret nodded. Moments like these reminded her how grateful she was that her mother persevered against James Blay Jr's demands and made certain she and Sadie could read and write.

William Blay stood outside his mother-in-law's room working up the courage to knock on the door. He put the back of his hand against the wood and tapped twice.

Catherine opened the door and offered William a generous smile as she motioned for him to come in.

Noticing how tired Margaret looked, he offered to take Maggie, who was still lying on the bed but not sleeping, Sarah and Susanna, outside to look at the boats in the harbour. 'Ours will be ready to board at 5 in the afternoon today,' he said to his wife. 'Our bags are with the porter. Come along girls. Maggie put your shoes on. We'll look at the boats.' Holding Susanna's hand, and making sure Sarah had hold of Maggie, William led the children into the streets of Hobart Town.

Catherine wiped a tear off her cheek.

'What is the matter, Mama?' Margaret asked.

'Your husband is the only Blay man left in Tasmania. Susanna will grow not knowing any of her relatives. It will be so different from when you were little.'

'There is nothing stopping you from coming to Port Phillip with us, Mama,'

'No, you will build a life there, and Sadie is in New Norfolk. Susanna and I will stay in Tasmania for now.'

'Do you think James will come for you and Susanna, Mama? Do you think he will write?'

'No. I don't. Once he had the money I got from selling the house, he lost interest in us. I have learned my lesson. It took twenty years, but I've learned it,' she smiled ruefully. 'I also learned not to declare all the cash in my possession.'

Margaret pushed herself out of the armchair and hugged her mother.

Caroline stirred as William and the girls made their way back into the room.

'It's time for us to pick up our things and make our way to the boat, girls.' William told his children. 'Give your Grandmama and Susanna a hug goodbye now, it might be busy on the wharf.'

Once again Margaret put her arms around her mother and hugged her. 'I will miss you, Mama.'

Catherine picked up Susanna and walked with her daughter, son-in-law and granddaughters to the street. She and the child waved as Margaret and her children followed William to the boat. When the tears rolled down her cheeks, she did not try to wipe them away.

10

BASS STRAIT

Bass Strait
"Currents in Bass Strait are predominately tidal in nature but are influenced by the South Australian Current (SAC), East Australia Current (EAC) and sub-Antarctic Surface Water (SASW). During the southern winter SASW is found widely present in the strait tracking from West to East. The warmer EAC is associated with the summer and autumn months and typically flows East to West in Bass Strait. These currents not only affect sea state, they can also affect local weather conditions, especially where there is mixing of the cooler currents with the warm EAC. These water patterns can combine with unusual pressure systems to create some alarming weather that whips up the sea surface."
https://oldsalt.net.au/passage-planning/bass-strait/>

"Bass Strait is a generally shallow (average depth of 50 m (160 ft)) stretch of water approximately 300 km (190 mi) wide and 200 km (120 mi) from north to south, encompassed by the entire northern coastline of Tasmania and Victoria's central to eastern coast. The prevailing winds and currents are westerly, the latter being divided by King Island, Tasmania at the western entrance to the strait, causing

unpredictable sea conditions, especially when strong winds occur.
For example, strong southerly winds can cause a strong northerly
current reflecting from the Victorian coast. The combination of
winds, currents, tidal flow and the shallow bottom often lead to tall
waves, often of short length, with a confused short swell often
conflicting in direction."
https://en.wikipedia.org/wiki/Bass_Strait_Triangle>

"The strait was named after George Bass, after he and Matthew
Flinders passed through it while circumnavigating Van Diemen's
Land (now named Tasmania) in the Norfolk in 1798–99."
https://en.wikipedia.org/wiki/Bass_Strait

January 1841.

E xasperated with the heat and the noise of her cranky children,
Margaret held onto the railing on the ladder leading up from
the sleeping and eating quarters on the boat and pulled herself up to
the deck. She didn't tell William. He could manage for five minutes.

Taking in deep breaths of the sea air, Margaret picked up the edge
of her apron and wiped her face. Other passengers were hanging on
to the railing and looking over the side of the boat. She didn't know
what they were marvelling at and didn't care. Tightening her cap so
the wind wouldn't run off with it, Margaret found a place to sit where
she could watch the sun set over what her husband told her was Bass
Strait. Changing from yellow to orange to red, the sun disappeared on
the horizon, leaving the space between daylight and darkness filled
with shades of grey and blue. Margaret put her hands on the bench
seat, pulled her body upright and made her way to the ladder and
back into the bowels of the boat. The putrid smell of vomit wafted
into her face, up her nose and down the back of her throat. Not
understanding what made people seasick, she thanked God for
sparing her the extra work. The rolling waves hadn't affected her girls
or her husband, and so far, she was free from the squirming stomach
that plagued many of the passengers.

The bunks allocated to the family for the one night and one-day trip to Port Phillip were tucked away at the back of the sleeping quarters. On first seeing their beds, Margaret was pleased to have a little more privacy than the other passengers, but with the stifling heat, the rollicking seas and the vomit she stepped over when she moved around the cabin, she ached to find a place on deck. With three small children and a husband on tenterhooks she would have to stay put.

One of the crew ventured into the vomit ridden sleeping quarters of the boat and lit the oil lamps, hanging them on hooks dotted around the edges of the space. Margaret preferred the darkness. The light brought the visibility of children with bile dried around their mouths, mothers pale with fatigue and their own seasickness, and fathers draped on bunks bemoaning their lot.

William helped settle the children into their bunk, Sarah down one end, and Maggie and Caroline up the other. The bunk underneath was too narrow for two adults, especially one whose sleep was disturbed by pregnancy. Margaret told William to go to bed, saying she would join him after another breath of fresh air. She sat on the end of the bunk until she heard the gentle snoring of the three girls in the bed above, then climbed up the ladder to the deck of the boat. The cool air wrapped around her cheeks reminding her of the times Grandmama Sarah Blay would hold her face in her hands and kiss it. Margaret touched a cheek and briefly closed her eyes, feeling Sarah's love.

Not alone in her desire to be out of the suffocating heat and smell of the sleeping quarters, Margaret had trouble finding somewhere to sit that would offer a little comfort. An older man, about the age she imagined James Blay Sr would be if he were still alive, offered her a seat on a wooden crate. It was lined up with others as makeshift seating, along the bow of the boat. Thanking the man, Margaret plonked on the crate, and loosened the ribbon holding her cap in place. Putting her head back and taking deep breaths to get more fresh air into her lungs, Margaret gasped at the majesty of the night sky. 'It's beautiful, amazing.' She wondered if this night sky, black as the charred wood that lay in the hearth when the fire was out and sparkling with stars, was a good omen for their new life in Port Phillip.

William opened his eyes. Turning to face the hand that was tapping his arm. He sat straight up 'What is it, Sarah? Where's Mama?' The six-year-old shrugged and wiped her hand under her nose, telling her father she felt sick and couldn't find Margaret. Pulling back the covers, William swung his feet out of the bunk and onto the floor. Careful not to hit his head on standing, he checked Maggie and Caroline. Both were sound asleep. 'Come here and sit with me on the bed,' he said to the little girl. 'Mama will be here soon.'

Sarah put her head on her father's lap and her legs on the bunk. He watched as she fought to keep her eyes open. Laying his eldest on the bed, her head on his pillow, William waited a few more minutes to make sure she was asleep. Pulling his boots and breeches on, he climbed up the ladder two steps at a time, to look for his wife.

Finding Margaret at the bow of the boat sitting on a wooden crate, her head bent back, her mouth open with drool dripping from its side, William panicked. He put his hands on her shoulders, shook them and called out her name.

Margaret's head bounced forward, her eyes sprung open and her mouth clamped shut. 'What? What?'

'You gave me a fright, Margaret, I thought you were sick like Papa when he had the apoplexy,' William whispered.

'Don't be stupid. I fell asleep.'

'Sarah woke saying she felt sick, I've put her in our bunk. You go down to her, and I'll stay here for a time. There isn't room in the bunk for two adults.' William helped his wife up from the crate and escorted her to the opening in the boat's floor that took them down into the floating oven.

Pushing Sarah over to the edge of the bed, so she was against the wall, Margaret took off her own shoes, cap and apron, and lay on top of the covers praying sleep would creep up and swallow her.

The gruel served for breakfast went uneaten by the passengers still struggling with seasickness. Margaret's children ate their own and some belonging to others who left plates untouched. William struggled to force the gruel into his mouth, but knowing dinner was some time away, made himself eat it. The smell and heat still affected Margaret. She couldn't eat.

'I have to go up on deck, William. I can't stay down here, I can't breathe. It's too hot.' Margaret complained.

William searched the quarters, looking under bunks, under chairs, on benches. 'What are you looking for?' Margaret asked.

'I need something to tie the girls together. Something strong enough to keep them safe, so they won't fall overboard. We can't expect them to stay down here until the boat arrives in Port Phillip. I'll ask a crew member.' William disappeared up the ladder.

'I've got something suitable,' William said as he bounded down the ladder. A sailor had given him two long, leather strips. William hadn't asked what they used them for. He tied one end of the strip to the ribbon that ran around the middle of Sarah's dress, and looped the other end through Maggie's dress. The middle of the strip was loose, so William could keep hold – a little girl at each end. He wrapped the other strip around Caroline's waist, tied it, and handed the end to Margaret. 'There,' he said. 'We can go onto the deck and all be safe.' His grin made the children giggle. Despite her fatigue, Margaret smiled.

Although not much room for the children to play, Margaret thought they were happier for being in the fresh air. The sea breeze that kissed their faces when they moved onto the deck in the morning, had turned into a nasty squall by dinner time. Sailors moved along, telling the passengers to get below. 'Bass Strait whips up nasty winds and currents,' one sailor remarked. 'Go below until we give the all clear.'

There was no all clear. Confined below deck for the rest of the journey they listened to each other vomit, dry-retch, moan and groan until the boat sailed out of the Strait into the bay that led to Melbourne.

11

WILLIAM

Port Phillip
"George Gipps became Governor of New South Wales in 1838. In
October 1839, he appointed Charles La Trobe as Superintendent of
the district. [Port Phillip] He was a gifted man with artistic and
scientific interests who did much to lay the foundations of
Melbourne as a real city. La Trobe's most lasting contribution to the
city was to reserve large areas as public parks: today these are the
Treasury Gardens, the Carlton Gardens, the Flagstaff Gardens, Royal
Park and the Royal Botanic Gardens.
A Separation Association had been formed in 1840 wanting Port
Phillip District to become a separate colony, and the first petition for
the separation was drafted by Henry Fyshe Gisborne and presented
by him to Governor Gipps. The entire population of Port Philip in
1841 was 11,738."
https://en.wikipedia.org/wiki/History_of_Melbourne

Melbourne 1841

Margaret waited until I helped her down the ladder which hung on the side of the boat so she could get into the tender. A fellow passenger kindly offered to hold on to Sarah, Maggie and Caroline. I didn't want them falling overboard after coming all this way. The little transport bobbed up and down with the swell from the bay while I climbed back up the ladder for the children. Caroline struggled to get out of my grip and bellowed for her mother. The bellowing continued even after I'd put her on Margaret's lap. With my supervision, Sarah held Maggie's hand and helped her down the ladder. Now that the family was ready for the last part of our journey to Melbourne, I collected our bags and set myself down next to my wife. The crew ordered more people on board which forced the passengers to sit closer together. Caroline objected and whined and cried for the twenty-minute journey from the boat to shore. My embarrassment evident, my face turned the vicious red of a fiery sunset.

I carried Margaret from the tender to the sand, helped her hold up her dress and carried her shoes as she waded through the shallows onto the shores of Port Phillip. Carrying Caroline who was still complaining about the whole affair, I managed to funnel Sarah and Maggie in front of me until they reached their mother.

Looking at my wife, my face flushed with the effort of manoeuvring the family to safety, I couldn't help the grin. 'We are here, Margaret. We are here.'

The feeble smile from Margaret gave me some encouragement 'We'll find a hotel straight away, and when you and the girls settle in the room we'll get something to eat.' I told her.

One of the sailors on the boat advised me to engage the services of a driver and his cart. I'm pleased I took the advice. It would have been impossible to walk with the luggage and the children to the hotel. After helping Margaret and the girls, I climbed up next to the driver and asked to go to a hotel in Collins Street. I couldn't remember the name, but I knew there weren't many, and I'd know when I saw it.

I wondered if Margaret noticed I hadn't performed my before bed routine on the boat, or in the hotel room. Kissing the children good-night, I climbed into the bed I would share with Margaret for the next couple of weeks. The girls piled into the second double bed on the other side of the room and went to straight to sleep.

I didn't sleep well. It wasn't because I was in a strange bed. It wasn't because the children were sleeping in the same room. It wasn't because Margaret tossed all night. I didn't sleep well because the excitement and trepidation of arriving in a new colony, of leaving our life behind in Van Diemen's Land, of the planning needed to start fresh, all rolled around in my mind from the moment I tried to close my eyes.

The rising sun forced its rays through the flimsy curtain that tried to shield the room's inhabitants from the increasing daylight. I was the only one awake. I slid out of bed, poured cold water from the pitcher into the washbowl on the sideboard and splashed my face. Sarah coughed. I stood still, holding my breath, I didn't want the children awake this early. With no more movement or noise, I dressed, and ran my hands through my hair. I didn't want to rummage through the bags looking for a hairbrush. Picking up my boots, I turned the knob on the door hoping it wouldn't squeak when I pulled it open. It was quiet.

In the hallway with boots in hand, and still no noise from the room, I bounded down the stairs. The same sun that forced its way into the room upstairs, didn't have an opportunity to envelop the dining room in light. The window curtains were drawn and although there was a smell of cooking from the kitchen beyond, the dining room oozed silence. I pulled on my boots, opened the front door of the hotel and stepped outside into the dusty, already hot, street. 'Hot, like Hobart.'

I pulled the piece of paper out of my shirt pocket that I'd written John's address on. My brother, John, had written to me as soon as he and Elizabeth and the children arrived in Melbourne. Following John's instructions, I walked up Collins Street, turned left into King, and then right into Bourke Street. John rented a small stone cottage about one hundred yards from the intersection. I didn't need to worry about choosing the right house; it was the only stone building at this end of Bourke Street.[1] I took off my hat and used it to dust off my shirt and breeches, then knocked on the door. While I waited for someone to answer, I wiped my hands on the front of my shirt to dry off the perspiration. My brother was in for a mighty handshake.

John opened the door just a little. I assume to see who it was knocking at such an early hour. On seeing me, he swung the door wide open, stepped out onto the dusty road, ignored my outstretched hand and wrapped his arms around my shoulders.

We hugged for a few moments before I pushed him away to look into the face I hadn't seen for two years. 'I've missed you, John.'

'And I you, brother. Come in, come in. We have another son to show you.'

John's wife, Elizabeth sat in a rocking chair next to the hearth of the unlit fireplace nursing an infant. Before I moved to greet Elizabeth, my eyes scanned the small cottage: two rooms, sparsely furnished, but clean. Two little boys played on the floor at the feet of their mother. Elizabeth welcomed me into their home, adding she would attend to refreshments when baby John had his fill.

I wasn't surprised to hear the child's name. The same names, in the same order, as my brothers' and mine. 'This must be James and William.' I patted the heads of my nephews, one born in March 1838, and one in December 1838, a few months before John and Elizabeth left Van Diemen's Land. 'Margaret is with child again,' I told my sister-in-law. 'She says this time we will have a son.' I smiled at the good fortune of my younger brother in having three sons, as our parents had.

As welcome as the refreshments were, I declined the offer from Elizabeth. Margaret didn't know where I was, so I thought it best to get back. I hugged John and we agreed both families should meet the coming Sunday.

For fear of becoming lost on the dirt roads that made up the town of Melbourne I retraced my steps back to the hotel in Collins Street, using John's instructions, in reverse order. I opened the door to the foyer, and ran up the stairs, two steps at a time. Turning the doorknob and opening the door into the room, my ears were assailed with Caroline's raucous bellowing, and Margaret's pleas with the child to be still. My family was awake.

Maggie held on to my hand, and Sarah hers, while my free hand carried a basket of foods prepared by the hotel kitchen. Margaret balanced Caroline on her left hip and lifted her dress up a little with the other hand to keep the hem from being painted brown with the dust on Collins Street. We waited for the horse and buggy I'd ordered.

My sister-in-law, Elizabeth, rushed to Margaret and hugged her for longer than Margaret was used to. Wiping tears from her eyes, Elizabeth ushered us into the kitchen of the little cottage. 'Come and sit at the table, I've made lemon drink. It is a pleasant drink for the summer.'

Margaret put Caroline on the floor with little James and William and sat down at the table.

'We have a small fenced garden at the back,' Elizabeth told Margaret. 'When they've had a drink, the children can play outside. I'll get dinner organised while John Jr is sleeping.'

Margaret seemed to enjoy Elizabeth's company; they were a year apart in age, and both with three small children. They didn't have much chance to get to know each other in New Norfolk. This might be good for my younger brother and me. If our wives get on, life will be happier.

The cousins, mine and Margaret's girls and John and Elizabeth's boys, played all afternoon, while the women caught up with the family news. John and I shared our plans. Both excited about our new start in a new colony.

Margaret thanked Elizabeth and John for the day, while I loaded the children into the buggy for the short trip back to the hotel in Collins Street. She told them we'd visit again, soon.

On our way back to the hotel, Margaret wanted to know where John was employed and if he could get me a position. She wasn't going to let me rest for too long.

I didn't want to work for someone else; I wanted to establish another farm.

12

FAMILIES

Education
"Education was poorly organised: in January 1840, only about 250 boys and girls attended the four church schools in operation. Religious leaders became concerned that young children without schooling would find themselves in positions of 'moral risk.' "

http://ergo.slv.vic.gov.au/explore-history/colonial-melbourne/everyday-life/population

"Until the building boom which followed the gold rushes, most of Melbourne was built of timber, and almost nothing from this period survives. Two exceptions are St James Old Cathedral (1839) in Collins Street (now relocated to King Street opposite the Flagstaff Gardens), and St Francis Catholic Church (1841) in Elizabeth Street."

https://en.wikipedia.org/wiki/History_of_Melbourne

Melbourne, 5th June 1841

Margaret's water broke just as she put the kettle on the fire to boil. William had left for work an hour earlier. The timber cottage they rented a few doors from John and Elizabeth in Bourke Street, hadn't warmed up from stoking the fire, but beads of perspiration dripped from Margaret's forehead, down her face, her neck and onto her bodice. 'This baby will not take long to come into the world.' Stooped with the pain of quick, intense contractions, Margaret went into the girls' bedroom to wake Sarah. The little girl sat up in bed, rubbed her eyes, and blinked at her mother. 'Sarah, put on your shoes and your coat and get Aunt Elizabeth. You stay with her boys while she comes to help Mama. Tell her the baby is coming.'

Without questioning, the seven-year-old grabbed her coat from the hook just inside the front door of the cottage and pulled her boots on.

Elizabeth had one-year-old John with her when she pushed open the door of the cottage. He looked as if he had just woken, and Margaret worried that he would wake Maggie and Caroline. Sitting the infant on the floor with a hard biscuit to suck, Elizabeth took Margaret's hand and led her to the bedroom. With a practised and calm manner Elizabeth helped her sister-in-law deliver her fourth baby girl.

'Poor William. He thought we would have a son in Port Phillip,' Margaret said.

'It seems we are destined to further the family line using a different path,' Elizabeth said as she cleaned up the sheets and blankets from Margaret's bed. 'What is to be her name?'

'Elizabeth, after my Grandmama.' Margaret lay back and held the infant to her breast just as Maggie and Caroline burst into the room. The little girls climbed up onto the bed to greet their new sister.

There would be no time to rest and get the new baby settled in Melbourne. Margaret's only companion was Elizabeth, and she was busy with her three boys. Seven-year-old Sarah must help look after Maggie and Caroline.

Elizabeth wrapped the new baby in swaddling and put her in her crib. 'I'll go home and see to the boys and send Sarah back. If you need help, send Sarah to tell me.'

Margaret pulled herself up on the pillows and thanked Elizabeth. This was the first baby she'd had where her mother wasn't a part of the delivery or the support afterwards. This time, she would be on her feet as soon as the girls were hungry. This time, her mother was miles away with a baby of her own. This time, there would be no help from an assigned convict housekeeper or cook. Apart from her sister-in-law, this time she was alone.

When William returned from working all day on the building site of a new church, St Francis Catholic Church in Elizabeth Street, Margaret was sitting in a chair by the fire nursing the infant. Maggie and Caroline sat at the kitchen table while Sarah cut slices of bread from a freshly baked loaf and trimmed portions of salted beef to put on their plates.

William grinned at his wife.

'Papa,' Maggie said. 'Mama had a baby this morning. Aunt Elizabeth came and helped her. The baby's name is Elizabeth, but not after Uncle John's Elizabeth, after Mama's Grandmama Elizabeth.'

William's shoulders slumped, and he took a deep breath before moving over to greet his wife and new daughter. 'How are you, my dear?' he asked Margaret. 'That was quick. Your pains hadn't started this morning when I left.'

'It was a shock, William. This child was in a hurry and she would not wait. I am thankful Elizabeth could help. Sarah looked after Elizabeth's boys while she was here. Sarah will delay starting school for a few weeks to help with the baby.'

The disappointment of another daughter hung over William's face like a shroud. Margaret was grateful he didn't say anything in front of the girls. As he leant forward to kiss her cheek and look at the baby, Margaret held his hand and squeezed. 'I know,' she said.

Unease exaggerated William's repetitive night-time behaviours. Margaret noticed he had added a few steps to his before bed ritual. The cause wasn't that she'd given birth to their fourth daughter; he had been like it since starting work on the building site. He'd complained he was a farmer not a builder.

Of the four girls, baby Elizabeth was the most placid. Margaret sent Sarah to the Church of England school earlier than planned because the infant either slept or lay awake in her crib watching her sisters. Margaret didn't need the help from her eldest daughter.

Although busy, Margaret missed her sister, Sadie, and her mother, Catherine. John's wife Elizabeth was her only friend, and they spent most days together. They shared their workloads. When one cooked, the other looked after the children. When one shopped, the other looked after the children. It was cheaper to hire one horse and cart for the trip to the market to buy both families supplies, than for each family to hire their own. While Sarah was at school Elizabeth's boys, James and William, played with Maggie and Caroline.

Margaret often wondered how different her life in Melbourne would be if not for Elizabeth Blay.

Christmas 1841

The Blay brothers worked together, lived near each other, and their wives had become close friends. The children kept each other company and Sarah, the only one attending school, tried to teach John's eldest James, and her sister, Maggie, to read and write.

Their wives were organising the first Christmas in the new colony: the two families would celebrate together.

Margaret, and Elizabeth who was expecting her fourth child, planned the Christmas Dinner for weeks. They baked cakes and buns, preserved fruit they bought from the market, picked vegetables they'd grown in their back gardens, carefully chosen perfect pieces of dried pork and beef, and each slaughtered a chicken. The feast was ready.

The rising sun on Christmas morning 1841 brought with it a

howling north wind that whipped up the dust on the barren, rutted, streets. Margaret got up at first light to feed baby Elizabeth, and to put the risen bread dough into the pan on the coals. She would leave the fire smoulder during the day so as not to heat the tiny cottage. Leaving the front door open to let in some air was out of the question; the north wind carried the dust, the heat and the flies into the house.

John and William carried Margaret's kitchen table into the back garden and collected more chairs from Elizabeth's kitchen. There was enough seating for everyone. The children organised themselves at the table and looked expectantly at their mothers for the feast to appear.

As Margaret carried plates of food for the families to share and enjoy, she remembered the Christmases in New Norfolk. They sat under the gum tree in the garden of Stoney Bank Farm: her mother, sister, grandmama, aunts, uncles and cousins, enjoying each other's company. She wondered if today would be the start of new traditions between the families. Her three older daughters and Elizabeth's three sons had a very strong cousin bond.

March 1842

Margaret tied baby Elizabeth's hat straps around her chin, heaved her onto her hip, and with a stern warning to six-year-old Maggie to take good care of Caroline, rushed to her sister-in-law's house two doors away. It annoyed her that Sarah was at school. Maggie wasn't as trustworthy.

At around ten o'clock Elizabeth's eldest, six-year-old James had run to ask Margaret to attend his mother. He didn't know why, just that his Mama needed Aunt Margaret's help and that it was very important. Margaret knew this meant Elizabeth was having the baby.

James had followed her back to the house. She put a blanket on the floor and lay baby Elizabeth down, telling James to watch her. Margaret was relieved the infant hadn't learned to sit up. She could imagine her toppling over on the hard, wooden floor and cracking her head.

Elizabeth Blay lay in her bed, arms behind her head, hands gripping the wooden slats that ran vertically down the bed head. Margaret rushed to her side whispering that everything would be all right. Elizabeth had the foresight to have water boiling on the fire, and to have a guard around the hearth so the small children were safe. Margaret put a cool cloth on her sister-in-law's brow and took the blankets and covers that would be hard to dry, off the bed. 'I'm here for you, Elizabeth,' Margaret said, 'like you were for me.' Pulling a chair in close to the bed, she wiped Elizabeth's forehead and face, thinking how frightened she looked. Supporting her through her pains, Margaret hurried between the bedroom and the kitchen and her own home, where she checked on the children. 'This is more difficult than in Van Diemen's Land, Elizabeth,' she said. 'There we had family support and assigned convicts to help with the house and the farm and the children.' Elizabeth nodded while the line of her clenched jaw tightened and the knuckles on her fingers turned white against the bedhead.

Elizabeth gave birth to a little girl[1] just as the children wanted their dinner. The baby didn't cry. She was limp, and blue. 'What's wrong?' Elizabeth pleaded.

Margaret wrapped the baby in a small blanket and handed her to Elizabeth. 'She is with the angels, Elizabeth,' Margaret said using every ounce of remaining strength not to weep. 'She was born that colour. The cord was around her neck.'

Elizabeth Blay let out a blood-curdling scream that caused baby Elizabeth to cry and three-year-old John to run out of the house into the street to his cousins.

After making Elizabeth physically comfortable, Margaret collected her daughters. Sarah was home from school and slicing bread for her sisters and cousin. 'Bring the bread Sarah, and pickles and the salted beef. Bring them to Aunt Elizabeth's place. She had a baby girl, but the infant is with the angels. We must look after the boys while Aunt Elizabeth rests.' Maggie and Caroline followed their mother out the door.

The cottage's kitchen wasn't big enough for six children and a six-month-old infant. Margaret handed baby Elizabeth to Sarah and told her to take the children into the garden to play while she prepared dinner. She made a cup of tea for Elizabeth, sliced the bread she had made the day before, spread pickles on a piece and took the drink and the food to her sister-in-law.

Elizabeth lay back on the pillows, cradling the dead newborn. All colour had drained from the woman's face and the tracks from torrents of tears ran down her cheeks. Except for her colour, the infant could have been sleeping.

Margaret touched Elizabeth's hand and put the tea and bread on the small cupboard next to the bed. 'You have something to eat, Elizabeth. The tea is hot. I'll take the baby and put her in her crib.' Margaret wanted to add that John could visit the chaplain when he got home but thought it best to let Elizabeth deal with the immediate tragedy without worrying about the next step.

Elizabeth relinquished the infant, picked up the cup of tea and watched as Margaret put the little girl in her crib.

Finding the cottage empty on his return from work, William went to his brother's. John stood by the fire, his back to the room, arms leaning on the chimney. Margaret was getting supper for all seven children. William walked to Margaret, leant in to her ear and asked what was going on. She took his hand and led him through the back door and into the garden. 'I helped Elizabeth with the delivery of a daughter, today. The child was born dead.' William put his arms around his wife and comforted her while she cried into his shoulder.

The pain Margaret felt for Elizabeth's loss penetrated her heart as if the child were her own. They all knew the chances of losing a baby at birth were high, just as the risk of losing a child at any age through disease or injury was high. It didn't make it easier.

With the emotion of the day behind her, Margaret got into bed thinking of Jessy Catherine, Aunt Sophia and Uncle William's baby, and how devastated her cousin Mary Rayner was when the baby died at six weeks of age. A child herself Margaret couldn't remember any feelings other than sadness. As a mother, sadness was an inadequate word to describe the loss.

William hesitated to follow his wife to bed. When he did, his routine became exaggerated and more repetitive. Margaret noticed. 'What is wrong, William? Something is bothering you.'

Climbing into bed next to his wife he said, 'I have bought 160 acres at a place called Greenhills on the River Plenty. We will move there and build a new life. Before you argue,' William put up his hand to stop Margaret speaking, 'John is taking his family to Geelong. We can't stay here. Neither John nor I want to labour on building sites. We are farmers.'

Margaret turned away from him, curled her knees up, wrapped her arms around them, and let the tears run down her face. She didn't make a sound.

'Did John say anything to you about moving away?' Margaret asked Elizabeth next morning. 'Yes. He announced last night that we are going to Geelong, and then perhaps to Portland. Oh, Margaret, we will be separated, just when we have become as close as sisters.'

September 1842

Margaret Blay and her sister-in-law Elizabeth settled Margaret's children into the wagon for the two-hour trip to Greenhills on the River Plenty. William had loaded their trunks on to the back where they would double as seats for the girls. Elizabeth and John would leave next year after the birth of their fifth child.

'I will write as soon as I can,' Margaret said. 'Please keep well and let me know when you have the baby.'

Elizabeth nodded, put her hands around Margaret's face and kissed her forehead. 'I will miss you very much my sister.'

13

WILLIAM'S NEW START

1

"Most Valuable Investment.
For Sale, one hundred and sixty acres of rich land, frontage to the River
Plenty, containing eight acres under cultivation, half wheat and the rest
potatoes, the latter crop alone valued at £100. Also, two capital dwelling
houses erected thereon: the whole to be sold in one or two lots.
The proprietor feels assured that this delightful estate needs only to be
inspected to insure its immediate purchase.
Terms very reasonable – further particulars can be known by application
to..."

Port Phillip Patriot and Melbourne Advertiser. 10 Jan. 1842.
(Trove.nla.gov.a)

"Houses that were planned were generally symmetrical, and very simple, usually containing 2 to 4 rooms around a central hallway. The kitchen was frequently detached and entered from a rear verandah or covered breezeway where pantry or scullery might also be located. Fireplaces projected outwards from the walls of the house..."

en.wikipedia.org/wiki/Australian_residential_architectural_styles# Victorian_Period_c._1840

Greenhills 1841-1842

The children were cranky and hungry by the time the horse and wagon I'd bought, and on which we all travelled, arrived on the 160 acre allotment at Greenhills.

After I helped Margaret down from the wagon, I got the girls out and set them on the ground, I left baby Elizabeth until last and handed the toddler to her mother. I really wanted Margaret's approval. This was a property where we could live until we departed this world. I looked at her, waiting for her to say something. The three eldest girls had already run off to investigate, forgetting their hunger and thirst.

Standing beside the wagon, still holding onto Elizabeth, I could see Margaret taking in the estate on the River Plenty. She noticed the gaps between the logs on the house had been filled with mud and commented that 'At least the draughts won't get in.' The front of the house had a small verandah and faced north; ideal for the colder months. 'There's a garden at the front. Is there a cleared area at the back of the house for vegetables and fruit trees?' she asked me.

'Put Elizabeth down and walk with me to see,' I answered. She took hold of Elizabeth's hand, and walked with me to the house. The front garden once had many flowers, but they seemed to have died over the heat of the summer. The garden at the back of the house was set up with rows of vegetables, and fruit trees. 'I think they are apples and pears,' I said to my wife. She smiled a tiny bit and then asked to see inside.

'Where is the furniture?' she demanded when she opened the door of the timber house.

'The property didn't come with furniture,' I said. 'I packed blankets for the first few nights. I'll go back to Melbourne to collect our furniture early next week.'

'If you had told me we were to sleep on a wooden floor with no comforts, I would have stayed in Melbourne until you had something ready for us.' Margaret raised her voice so much that one-year-old Elizabeth hid behind my legs.

All I wanted was for her to like it. Yes, there was work to do, but it was a good property. There were two houses on it. We would live in one and the workers could stay in the other. The stable was sound. There were trees outside for shade and the girls wouldn't all have to sleep in one room. I was upset by her response. 'It won't take long to get the furniture and get the house organised, this is a nice house and it's in a wonderful location.' I turned and went outside so she wouldn't see how upset I was with her reaction.

From outside I watched as Sarah, Maggie and Caroline ran through the front door into the hallway calling for their mother.

'Mama, there is a garden out the back with lots of vegetables, and fruit trees,' Sarah told her. 'There's some wheat growing and potatoes, and the river is easy to get to for water.'

While she didn't think I could hear, Margaret told the girls about the inside of the house. 'There are three bedrooms, so you won't all have to sleep in the same one,' she said 'and there is a separate kitchen out the back, so the fire won't make the house hot in summer, and there's a parlour and a dining room. There is plenty of space for us. Papa will bring in your things, but you won't be able to unpack until he gets the furniture.'

'Where will we sleep if there's no beds?' Sarah asked.

'I don't know, yet.' I heard Margaret say. At least she didn't complain to the children about sleeping on the floor.

When I took our belongings off the wagon, I put them in the appropriate rooms. I dragged the girls' trunk into one bedroom and mine and Margaret's into the other. Sending Sarah and Maggie to collect firewood from the woodshed at the back of the house, I told them to stack it in the wood barrel in the kitchen. Better to keep them busy, I thought.

Unharnessing the horse, I led it under a tree out of the glaring spring sun and asked Margaret to get some water from the river for the horse and the kettle. I still had much to unpack from the wagon. The river was just over the rise, not far. The girls had found it earlier.

'Just how do you think I will be able to carry water for a horse, and a kettle, with a three-year-old and a one-year-old hanging on to me?' Margaret huffed. 'I'll help Sarah and Maggie while you get the water.' She took hold of Caroline's and Elizabeth's hands, and marched toward the older girls who had firewood stacked in a pile. It seems I'll be getting the water.

Margaret and the girls did fill the wood barrel in the kitchen, but there were other chores that needed attending to. I decided not to bother asking for help.

I knew she was annoyed with me. I knew she missed her mother and sister, and I knew she hadn't wanted to move away from Elizabeth. They'd become close and relied on each other. But we had to build a future, and that future was here in River Plenty. Besides it was a beautiful location, much more pleasant than dusty, smelly Melbourne.

I watched as she walked with the girls. They picked wildflowers, chased butterflies, ran after magpies that were bigger than the Van Diemen's Land magpies, and rolled in the grass. When I heard Caroline's complaints about being hungry and thirsty I knew the frolicking would end.

By the time they all got back to the house I had the kitchen packed with our supplies and food stores. I was hot and red-faced, and to stop the perspiration from running down my face I'd tied a kerchief around my head. I was filling a trough with the water I'd collected in buckets from the river and wondered if Margaret felt at all guilty when she noticed the horse had a bucket of water at its feet.

She went into the kitchen to prepare something for dinner, and tasked Sarah with starting a fire in the fireplace.

Margaret appeared to appreciate the effort I'd gone to in arranging wooden crates into seats that framed the edges of an old barrel I found in the stable. The barrel would do as a table for now. She found the food items stored in crates, in order of freshness. I stacked the dried meats high, followed by flour, oatmeal and corn-meal. The four loaves of bread Margaret had made before we left Melbourne, and some hard biscuits were in a crate under the flour. Next level down were the vegetables she'd picked from the garden at our rented cottage in Bourke Street, with potatoes and onions sitting in a crate on the floor. As organised as I was, I knew we wouldn't be able to live on potatoes and wheat. There was a lot to be done.

Margaret prepared a small meal for our family. She used almost a whole loaf of bread, setting it on a plate on the barrel alongside pickles and some salted pork. Sarah had a good fire going, and the previous owners had left the frame for the kettle, which Margaret put on to boil.

Despite her reservations, I think Margaret appreciated why I thought Greenhills would be a good place to begin a new life. The house was in a natural clearing, a hundred yards walk from a sparkling, clean stream which was the River Plenty. The air, clear and fresh with the smells of the trees and earth, reminded me of New Norfolk, and the dirt appeared easy enough to till.

'What are your plans, William? How long before we have the furniture and can start settling in? she asked while we were eating.

'Establishing the farm is a priority,' I told her. 'We must plant more vegetables and fruit trees, or we won't have enough to eat. We'll get started over the next few days. I'll go to Melbourne next week to buy goats, pigs and chickens, and collect the furniture. I'm going to hire two workers to help us get established.'

'Do we have enough money to pay labourers?' Margaret asked.

'I have the money from the sale of Stoney Bank Farm but will need half for supplies and workers. I've paid the other half as a deposit on these 160 acres; the bank will provide the balance.'

I noticed Margaret's fists squeeze by her sides, her jaw tightened, lines gathering on her forehead as she glared at me. 'I didn't know you were borrowing money again,' she said between clenched teeth.

'You do not need to know. I have everything under control.' I told her.

Sarah looked after Caroline and Elizabeth while Maggie and Margaret got the girls' bedroom ready for their first night in Greenhills. The child helped spread a large canvas sheet on the floor to stop the draughts from the boards making them cold. Tonight, they would all be sleeping on the floor, on the mat. I sorted out Margaret's and my bedroom with another canvas mat.

While I made my way back to the house after performing my abolitions, I noticed Margaret standing on the front verandah. She put her head back and looked up at the stars-the same stars as in New Norfolk-she smiled. When I reached her, she put her arm in mine and led me inside. I think this meant she was warming to the idea of living at River Plenty, on this, our Greenhills.

The girls were too tired to argue about eating, washing, and going to bed on the floor and had gone straight to sleep. Margaret and I sat on the wooden crates in the kitchen and stared at the kettle hanging on the frame, waiting for it to boil. We didn't speak. Perhaps she was tired. I knew there was no point moving towards her and putting my arm around her. She wouldn't be amenable to making love on a wooden floor.

Not being able to complete my night-time routine left me flummoxed. I tried to hide it from Margaret. There wasn't any hot water to wash with, I didn't have a rag and salt to clean my teeth, and there was nowhere to put my clothes in readiness for the morning. It was too dark to look in the trunk for my nightshirt, so I slid under the blanket, and lay on the floor, in my underwear. The enormity of the tasks ahead made me anxious and caused a fitful sleep.

'We can't wait until next week, William. You must at least get our beds, today. The other furniture can wait. You have improvised, and we'll manage, but we are all tired from very little sleep and our bodies ache. The girls and I can't help with the farm if we are in pain.'

That's how I was greeted as soon as Margaret got up and came into the kitchen. I'd been up for at least two hours and had fed the horse and finished unpacking the wagon. I was putting water on for the oatmeal.

As annoyed as I was at being expected to go to Melbourne again so soon, I knew she was right. I hadn't slept the night before; I couldn't get comfortable and the hard, wooden floor dug into my hips. Not sleeping gave my mind the opportunity to fret over the amount of work required to get the farm producing enough surplus to sell, and to worry about whether my money would last.

Taking the food Margaret packed for me, I harnessed the horse, and waved to the family as I made my way to the track that led to Melbourne.

Christmas 1842 – Green Hills

Margaret had asked me to take the family to Melbourne for Christmas. She missed Elizabeth and said the girls would like to see their cousins. I refused. I didn't have time for the journey. There was so much to do. I told her we'd go in the new year.

This Christmas day the temperature climbed quickly. The children used a bucket to collect fresh water from the river and sat under a big gum tree dipping their mugs into the bucket and drinking the cool liquid while Margaret, sweeping her arms to keep the bush flies out of her eyes and off the food, prepared a special dinner. The chickens I brought back from one of my trips to Melbourne were wonderful layers. There were plenty of eggs, but we'd decided to slaughter one of them for Christmas. Margaret prepared the chicken and put it in the dutch oven early in the morning, buried in the coals to cook. The pig, which would now have been of a size to slaughter and eat, escaped a week after arriving. We sometimes heard it in the bush but had never been close enough to catch it. Margaret made cheese from the milk the goat produced and would spread this on some fresh bread. My mouth watered while she organised our dinner.

Watching my daughters' excitement over the treats Margaret had prepared for Christmas Dinner, I wondered if things would be easier if Sarah had been a boy. I would now have help setting up the farm. The two labourers who followed me back from Melbourne on my first trip, had helped with new fencing, and ploughing but disappeared after their first payday. I hadn't had time to look for more on any subsequent trips. I would in the New Year. I needed help on the farm. A surplus would provide income.

January 1843

I kept my promise and took Margaret and our four daughters on my next trip to Melbourne, leaving at sunrise on a Wednesday in January. Margaret was more excited than the children. The early start, needed to avoid the extreme heat of the day, saw us arrive in Bourke Street around eight in the morning. I wasn't staying in Melbourne. After securing workers I would return to Greenhills at first light Thursday. Leaving the chickens and the goat alone worried me. We'd lost the pig, losing the goat and any of the chickens would be catastrophic. Funds were running low, there wasn't enough to replace any livestock that vanished into the bush.

Bourke Street 1843

Margaret didn't wait for me to help her from the wagon, she hoisted up her skirts, clambered off and embraced Elizabeth with such gusto the little boy standing next to his mother, stepped away. The women hugged for a long time, then stepped back to take in the appearance of each other.

'It's been less than a year,' Margaret said 'but seems like an eternity. I have been so lonely.'

She hadn't told me she was lonely. How did she have time to be lonely?

'Come inside out of the sun, take refreshments, and clean yourselves up.' Elizabeth said. She ushered Margaret and the girls into the cottage, making her three sons, James five, William four, and John almost three, stand aside to let their cousins pass. 'John is working,' she told me.

The two friends left the children to sort out their own games and sat at the kitchen table catching up on each other's lives. I pretended to be occupied with the horse but managed to catch parts of their conversation. 'You are strong, Margaret, and patient,' Elizabeth said 'and William is more thorough and calculated than John. John would have given up, sold the land and moved away to start again somewhere else.'

I was encouraged to hear that., but I doubted my younger brother would ever give up.

'You are looking tired,' Margaret said, 'are you keeping well with this baby?'

Elizabeth took my wife's hands and pulled her in close across the table. I moved nearer to the door to listen.

'I think this one is a girl, but I won't say anything to John. This one is very different. I have been sick all along, some days it's hard to keep any food down, she kicks all day and complains at night if I lie on my side too long, and my feet swell. However, it will all be a blessing if I have another girl. One that survives.'

'Are there any midwives in Melbourne?' Margaret asked

Elizabeth assured her there were a number, and as the population was young, they were in high demand. She had paid a deposit and secured the services of an experienced midwife for March. 'I hope I don't go into April.'

The rest of their conversation was about children and gardening, so I didn't listen. I led the horse to the back of John's place – he didn't have a stable – and secured the wagon. I'd buy supplies and head back at first light tomorrow.

I picked up my family one week after leaving them at my brother's. I'd secured the services of two workers who seemed trustworthy. I'd left them at the farm to keep working on the ploughing, while I took the wagon to Melbourne to collect Margaret and the children.

Embracing Margaret on the street outside John's house, my face turned as red as the angry sunsets in the middle of summer.

'Pull your shirt out of your breeches for a little while, William,' Margaret whispered, 'we don't want the children to see.' She kissed my cheek, knowing the shirt would have to be loose for a little longer.

The cousins hugged and said goodbye. Margaret and Elizabeth didn't speak to each other, it seems they'd said all they needed to before this moment. I helped Margaret onto the seat next to me, and John lifted my girls into the back of the wagon. They sat amongst the supplies of food and building materials I'd purchased. The children waved until everyone was out of sight.

March 1843

I always visited John and Elizabeth on my trips to Melbourne. The trip on 30th March left me elated, and excited to get home to tell Margaret the news. Three days earlier, on 27th, Elizabeth gave birth to a little girl, Elizabeth Comet Blay. The arrival of the infant helped to heal the wounds left by the birth of the stillborn daughter two years earlier.

As I was preparing to return to Greenhills, I asked my brother the meaning of the newborn's middle name, *Comet*.

'It means *origin* apparently,' said John. 'It's a name Elizabeth has saved for a girl. It's a family name. As soon as Elizabeth and the infant are strong enough, we are leaving for Geelong,' he added. 'I'll write to you when we are leaving.'

I shook hands with my brother, hugged him and looked into his eyes, wondering if we would see each other again.

14

GREENHILLS, RIVER PLENTY

"Road to the River Plenty. – We perceive that a notice is given for a Meeting of parties interested in the formation of a road form Melbourne to the River Plenty via Heidelburgh, a project which we trust will be carried into effect."

[1]

27 September 1843

Margaret's water broke while she was getting Elizabeth dressed. The little girl was just over two-years-old and still the quietest and most placid of her children. Looking at the pool of water between her mother's feet, Elizabeth laughed and said, 'Wee wee.'

'Sarah,' Margaret called to her eldest, 'I need you.'

Hurrying into Elizabeth and Caroline's bedroom pulling her dress over her head, Sarah stopped, mouth agape. 'What's wrong, Mama?'

'My water has broken, Sarah. That means the baby is on its way. It won't be long. Find Papa or one of the workers and have them send for the midwife. Come back as soon as you can.'

Between contractions, Margaret put towels on the bed, and put more wood on the fire so the water would boil. She staggered to the bedroom, holding the walls for support, lay on the bed trying not to scream or groan too loudly. She didn't want to frighten the children.

Sarah told Maggie to take care of Caroline and Elizabeth while she sat with their mother. 'It'll be all right, Mama,' Sarah soothed. The seven-year-old's face belied her words of comfort. Her jaw was gritted tight, her brow furrowed, and her hands sweaty.

Within an hour of her water breaking, Margaret knew the baby would be born with the aid of a seven-year-old child. William had sent for the midwife and then returned to his work on the farm. 'Sarah,' she said to her eldest, 'the baby is coming, you must help it come out, then give it to me.'

Nodding, Sarah lost all colour in her face, and moved to the end of the bed. 'I can see it, I can see it,' she yelled.

Using all her strength, Margaret gave an almighty push to deliver the child. Sarah guided the newborn into the world and gave it to her mother.

'It's a boy, Mama,' she said. 'We have a baby brother.'

'He needs to cry, Sarah,' Margaret whispered, 'pat his back.'

Obeying her mother's instructions, the little girl picked up the baby, held him to her, and patted his back with her free hand.

'Harder,' Margaret said.

She put more force into the rhythm and a few moments later the infant cried with his first breath of air. Sarah grinned.

Margaret talked Sarah through cutting the cord, cleaning the baby, and wrapping him in a blanket. She explained about the after-birth, and when all the events related to the birth of a child were done, Margaret put her new baby boy to her breast, beaming at Sarah. 'Thank you.'

The midwife arrived with the worker William had sent to collect her. Embarrassed to walk in on Margaret feeding the baby, the worker tipped his hat, apologised and said he would find 'Mr William.'

'You look well, Mrs Blay,' the midwife said, 'and Sarah, you have performed a task usually left for grown women. Your Mama will be proud of you.'

The seven-year-old smiled and helped the midwife clean up the towels and Margaret to get out of bed. 'I'll check that Maggie is looking after my sisters,' she said as she left the room.

William bounded through the kitchen, into the hallway, and into the bedroom sounding like the horse when its hooves clopped over the rocks on the track to Melbourne. 'You've had the baby, already? What is it? Are you well?'

It didn't go unnoticed by Margaret or the midwife that William's concern for his wife came after the question about the baby's gender. 'You have a son, William,' Margaret said, 'a son'.

William knelt next to the chair Margaret sat in. He touched the baby's head with one hand and wiped the tears from his cheeks with the other. Smiling at Margaret, he said 'His name is William James. William James Blay.' [2]

Name	William James Blay
Gender	Male
Baptism Age	0
Birth Date	27 Sep 1843
Baptism Date	17 Nov 1843
Baptism Place	St. James, Melbourne, New South Wales, Australia
Residence Date	1843
Residence Place	New South Wales, Australia
Father	William Blay
Mother	Margaret

Margaret wanted to share the news of her baby son with Elizabeth and John but with the founding of a small town at River Plenty, William did not need to travel to Melbourne as often. A mail run, established between Melbourne and River Plenty, would take a letter.

Dear Elizabeth,

I pray this letter finds you, John and your children well. Much to William's happiness, we have a son, born on 27 September. His name is William James. I am well, and he is a strong, demanding, infant. He will be baptised at St James on 17 November, please say you will be able to come. William said you and John are going to Geelong, I hope you can delay that journey until the baptism. You and John are to be William James' godparents.
I look forward so much to seeing you again.

With much love and affection,

Margaret

The baptism of William James Blay also served as a goodbye to Elizabeth and John and their children. Margaret's head pounded from the anxiety of her friend moving even further away. Smiling and being gracious to the minister, and her guests, Margaret camouflaged the pain in her head, the pain that reflected the fear of no close family within reach.

William's happiness at having a son spread to his feet. He bounced around with his son in his arms. He showed him off to the minister and his brother and sister-in-law.

Margaret wondered if his face was aching from all the smiling he was doing.

Taking Elizabeth aside, Margaret made her promise to write often. 'If the farm does well and we have money to spare, we could even catch a steamboat and visit you,' Margaret said. 'Or you can visit us.'

'Yes, the travel would be possible on a boat,' Elizabeth said, 'much quicker than a bumpy coach journey.'

With the families saying their final goodbyes, Margaret and William headed home to Greenhills, the sun at their backs, the baby on Margaret's lap, and the girls chatting in the back of the wagon.

The pain of grief in Margaret's head pounded in time with the horse's clopping on the recently excavated road.

15

MARGARET BLAY

Crutches
"The first evidence of their use dates back to the time of the
Pharaohs, clearly visible in a carving dating to nearly 3000 BCE. The
earliest crutches were essentially a T-shaped design, which slowly
morphed into the more popular V-shape in use today. They were
made form a piece of hardwood cut to length and split near the top to
create this V-shape. A wooden underarm piece could then be
attached for both underarm and handle use. Although
uncomfortable as they lacked cushioning, they proved effective."

https://bonesurgeon.com.au/crutches-history

1844-1845

The worker, whose name Margaret hadn't bothered to
remember, ran to the house and banged on the kitchen door
with his fists. Annoyed at the intrusion into her day, Margaret wiped
flour off her hands and marched to the door ready to give the worker
a reprimand. On seeing his face, Margaret took a quick breath 'What?
What is it? What's happened?'

'It's Mister William, Missus Blay. He tripped when he was ploughing the field and spooked the bullocks. He was dragged along a fair way, we think his leg's broken.'

Margaret looked around the kitchen for an answer to the question she hadn't yet formulated in her head. 'Has anyone gone into town for the doctor?' she eventually asked.

'Yes, Missus Blay, Tom's gone to get the doctor. We'll need to bring Mr William to the house, but I need help to put him on the wagon.'

Again, Margaret looked around the kitchen for an answer. She stood for a few moments. 'Sarah, Maggie and Caroline are at school, the new Church school, they've only been going a few weeks. What will I do about Elizabeth and William James?'

'Missus Blay?' the worker prodded.

'Oh, yes. Harness the horse to the wagon. I'll have to bring the children. William James is too naughty to leave with Elizabeth,' she grumbled to herself.

Taking off her apron, Margaret packed some biscuits for William James into a calico bag and gave it to Elizabeth to carry. With the five-year-old girl following behind, she slung William James onto her hip and hurried to the stable.

Her husband lay in a freshly ploughed furrow. His eyes were closed, and Margaret despaired he had died. 'William, William,' she called as she climbed down from the wagon, leaving William James and Elizabeth in the back. Kneeling beside her husband, she picked up his head, and put the jacket the worker had offered, under it. William opened his eyes, gave a feeble smile, then screwed up his face as a jab of pain shot through his leg. His breeches were torn, and Margaret could see the blood, and gouges in his skin from being dragged on the dirt.

'We have to get you on the wagon, William. It will be painful, but we must get you home.'

William nodded.

The worker put his arms under William's shoulders and dragged him as close to the wagon as possible. William's eyes stayed closed, with his mouth clamped shut and his fists in a tight ball. The worker climbed into the back of the wagon, lay on his belly, leaned right down and again put his arms under William's shoulders. Standing to one side, Margaret put her arms under William's knees. Mustering the strength she reserved for childbirth, she ignored her husband's screams, and helped the worker manoeuvre him into the wagon. Elizabeth sat quietly, with a frown on her forehead. Two-year-old William James tried to climb on his father. Margaret got between her husband and son to stop the toddler.

'We'll leave you in the wagon until the doctor gets here,' Margaret said. 'It might not be as painful with three men moving you.' He didn't answer. Lifting the two children from the wagon, she went into the house to get a cup of water for her husband. Elizabeth stayed in the house while William James followed along behind his mother back to the wagon. It was a struggle to get her husband to take a little of the water.

The three older girls arrived home from school to the screams of their father. Sarah told Maggie and Caroline to wait outside, while she rushed in. Margaret stopped her in the kitchen, explaining what had happened. 'Tell Maggie and Caroline to come in,' she said. 'The three of you stay here and look after Elizabeth and William James. I'll see if the doctor needs assistance.'

William lay on their bed, his face the colour of the ash in the hearth. His breeches had been cut off and thrown on the floor, the damp blood leaving marks on the rug. 'Mrs Blay,' the doctor said, 'please bring in more boiled water and clean rags.' Margaret hurried to obey, not wanting any delay of hers to cause her husband more distress.

William passed out as the doctor manipulated the bones in his leg to realign them before applying a splint. 'This happens,' he explained. 'The pain is too intense to bare, and the patient succumbs to unconsciousness. I did not have any laudanum in my bag, and this could not wait.'

Margaret was at a loss to understand how a doctor could attend a patient with a broken bone and carry no pain relief. 'I could have given him whisky,' she said, 'if you'd asked.'

'I have whisky,' said the doctor 'I used it to clean the wounds.'

Saying Margaret could pay his fee when he came back in a few days to check on William, the doctor climbed into his buggy, flicked the whip onto his horse's back, and stirred up a cloud of dust as he left Margaret and her children to look after the farm and William.

Sinking into an ocean of melancholia, William had difficulty getting out of bed, and toileting, washing, dressing were almost impossible tasks. He relied on Margaret more and more. The doctor said it would be three months before he could remove the splint from his leg.

Margaret kept Sarah home from school to help with the household chores and the younger children. Without William to push the labourers to work, little was being done.

———————————

With the splints removed from William's leg, the doctor provided a pair of crutches. Moving around the house, the vegetable garden and orchards was manageable, and William coped with getting to, and cleaning out the stable. Working on the paddocks: ploughing, sowing, harvesting, were tasks beyond his current capability. The anxiety associated with the farm's deterioration and his damaged leg, saw a resurface of the repetitive behaviours William had tried so hard to keep under control. The physical hindrance of his still painful leg, the disappearance of the two workers once Margaret had given them a month's pay, the workload associated with the house and farm, and the lack of income from produce to sell, sent William into a spiral of despair.

———————————

After William and Margaret loaded as much of their furniture as would fit on the wagon, William harnessed the horse. Sitting wherever they could find a space, the five children squeezed onto the back with the furniture. Margaret sat up front with William. She wiped tears as they drove away from Greenhills. The bank had taken possession; and left them with nothing. This baby would be born in Melbourne, not on the farm in River Plenty that she thought would see out her days.

William didn't hurry the horse. The road had been excavated and the journey to Melbourne took less time than it used to. He had secured rent on a cottage in Collingwood. He would sell the horse and wagon and look for work as soon as they arrived.

16

COLLINGWOOD

Collingwood

"Collingwood and Fitzroy were first known as Newtown, Melbourne's earliest suburb, and 25-acre (10 ha) blocks were offered for sale there in 1838. Only a handful of blocks along the Yarra River were settled by the early 1840s. In 1842, Newtown was renamed Collingwood by Robert Hoddle on instructions from Superintendent La Trobe, possibly after the Collingwood Hotel which bore the name of the British admiral who succeeded Nelson at Trafalgar. East Collingwood stretched from the sloping ground of Smith Street in the west and Heidelberg Road in the north, dropping sharply to boggy, low-lying ground that extended to the Yarra River in the east and present-day Victoria Street in the south. Some of the higher ground was subdivided in the 1840s, but the real rush to fill the Collingwood Flat occurred in the 1850s."

http://www.emelbourne.net.au/biogs/EM00375b.htm

"The earliest school in the area was established for Aboriginal children in the 1840s but the rapid influx of working-class families,

many of them immigrants, resulted in a need for formal European
style schools by the early 1850s."
http://makingfutures.net/schools-and-communities/collingwood/
collingwood-history-of-schooling

"Infant mortality was very great and the Health Officer's reports for
years were of the prevalence of scarlet fever, diphtheria, dysentery,
and other zymotic diseases due to bad drainage and lack of sewerage
— diseases, however, not then peculiar to Collingwood, or the "Flat".
In 1861 ten per cent of all Collingwood children under 5 died."

http://collingwoodhs.org.au/wp-content/uploads/3-Early-Collingwood-
Memories-In-Those-Days.pdf

1845

The house in Collingwood closely resembled the cottage they
lived in in Bourke Street, down from John and Elizabeth: two
bedrooms, a parlour, and a kitchen set inside the house. Margaret
missed the house at Greenhills. Having the kitchen separate from the
house was a blessing in the hot summer months when the heat from
the cooking stove stayed out of the parlour and bedrooms. The five
children shared a room. When this baby was born, six would be in
the one room. Sarah complained as soon as they arrived. There was
no drainage from the house, residents had to dig their own. They
must collect water in tanks and bucket it into the house. At least there
was an established vegetable garden.

With no school at Collingwood Margaret set aside part of the day
to teach Sarah, Maggie and Caroline, writing, reading, and numbers.
The girls' domestic education was continuous. One of the most
important tasks, making candles. Without candles, they could
achieve nothing after dark unless one sat in front of the fire. In
summer that was not a pleasant option. [1]

Margaret remembered how she and Sadie worked in the
vegetable garden at her Papa's house in Hobart Town and then at the

houses they lived in in New Norfolk. Using the information her mother passed to her, she taught the three older girls about growing food. She taught them to recognise when potatoes were ready to dig up, how to check if carrots were ready to pull out of the ground and when the corn ears were right to pick. Three-year-old Elizabeth kept baby William busy.

Watching Sarah with her sisters, Margaret felt a twinge of sadness creep into her heart. At Sarah's age Margaret was besotted with William and had determined to marry him. Sarah could be married in five or six years. Shaking her head to rid it of the melancholia, Margaret left the girls to tend the garden, and picked up William James who was fussing and grizzling. Little Elizabeth followed along behind her mother. 'How can two children be so different? Elizabeth is gentle, easy going, and William James is cranky, demanding and difficult.' Margaret shrugged her shoulders to no one and took the two youngest into the house.

When Margaret bent over to put William James on the floor, a wave of nausea enveloped her. Holding her hand over her mouth she rushed outside as far away from the house as possible. Everything she'd eaten during the day spread out over the dirt, not far from the potatoes the girls had dug up.

Sarah rushed to her side 'Mama, you are sick. Come and sit down.'

'It's all right, Sarah. I'll be fine. Just an upset stomach.' She wiped her mouth with the end of her apron and went inside to see what William James was doing. 'Please God, don't let me be with child,' she muttered.

John Douglas Blay was born on 22nd November 1845. The heat in the bedroom was suffocating. Margaret begged Sarah to get cold water from the tank to both drink and wipe her face and head. Sarah had helped Margaret with the delivery of this baby, just as she had with William James. But this time the eleven-year-old supported her mother, delivered the baby, cut the cord, wrapped him in a blanket and handed him to her mother for his first feed. Nine-year-old Maggie took care of the other children.

'He is very quiet, Mama,' Sarah said, a furrow on her brow contradicting her years. 'He isn't screaming like William James did. He doesn't look very strong, either.'

Realising Sarah was right, she held the baby away from her to take in his appearance. Although his skin didn't have the same blue tinge that Jessy Catherine's had until the day she died at four weeks and thirteen days, he was not a normal colour. He didn't have the same presence a newborn had. Knowing there was no money to spare for a doctor, or even a midwife, Margaret would keep praying that her second son would survive.

William was as excited at the birth of his second son as his first. 'We will have boys, now,' he said, holding the infant in his arms.

'I don't know why boys are so important to you, Papa,' Sarah said. 'We girls do more work around here than any boy would.' Flouncing out of the bedroom with the pile of towels marked with the evidence of childbirth, Sarah slammed the door in her wake, as if showing her strength to her father.

'She is right, William,' Margaret said. 'And this little boy doesn't seem as well as our other children have been. His presence reminds me of Aunt Sophia's baby, Jessy Catherine. Do we have money for a doctor?'

William pulled the blanket away from the baby's head. 'He looks just fine. You feed him, and he'll be as strong as William James. We are calling him John Douglas Blay. John after my brother, and Douglas because I like it.' Handing the newborn back to his mother, William opened the bedroom door, leaving his wife to worry about the infant's health on her own.

While she was getting dinner ready for the children, one of the neighbour's workers knocked on the door with a letter he'd collected on his visit to town. It was from Elizabeth Blay. Margaret gave William James an apple to attack while she read the letter.

Dear Margaret

The children are all well, as I hope are yours. I'm not with child and to be honest am finding the liberation quite beneficial to my health. John has moved us from Geelong to Portland. It is about 220 miles from Melbourne. It's a long way. It took us five weeks to get here on the bullock wagon. John has purchased land and is establishing a farm. He is already becoming involved in the local community.

There is a school here, so James and William attend each day. John Jr is learning how to garden and look after the animals. He will go to school when he is six.

I am kept busy establishing a vegetable garden and managing the other household requirements, you will know what I mean. John has employees working on the farm. He often says he doesn't understand why Port Phillip was not a convict colony like Van Diemen's Land; there is plenty of work to be done.

I will need to find more paper to write to you in the future, this piece is too small.

I love you, and miss you, and hope we see each other again soon.

With love

Elizabeth

Margaret folded up the letter and tucked it into the bosom of her dress. She didn't want to share it with William. Wiping her eyes, she felt a pang of jealousy trickle into her heart. John was industrious, settled, reliable. He reminded Margaret of her father-in-law, James

Blay Sr. William couldn't manage money or be successful for a sustained period.

Waiting until William was already in bed, so she didn't have to witness his ritual, Margaret washed her face, brushed her hair and changed into her nightdress. 'I have news to share with you, William,' she said as she slid under the covers 'Elizabeth wrote to tell me she and John and the children have moved to Portland. It's over 220 miles from Melbourne. I hope we can go on a boat to visit them one day.' She looked across for a response from her husband.

'It will be some time,' he said. 'I was fined in court today and ordered to pay costs.'

Margaret waited, but her husband said no more. She rolled over, her back to him, wondering if they could ever be as settled as John and Elizabeth.

"Monday last, a man named William Blay appeared on summons before the Mayor, charged by Mr. Jonathan Ryder of the Plenty....when the defendant rode up, and, springing from his horse, threw the complainant heavily to the ground, remounted his horse and drove them off. The Bench fined the defendant £3 3s 2d for the assault, and £1 16s 10d costs."[2]

17

CATHERINE

Tasmania

"There was ample employment for women as servants, but while scarcity of servants meant wages rose to a certain extent, domestic service remained menial."

*http://www.utas.edu.au/library/
companion_to_tasmanian_history/G/Gender.htm*

Hobart, Tasmania, 1847

Catherine's eight-year-old daughter Susanna was head-strong, self-centred and belligerent, like her father. The child ran wild in the streets of Hobart, refused to attend school, and changed her name, depending on her mood. Some days she was Susanna Sarah, her birth name. Other days she was Susan Elizabeth or Susanna Elizabeth, and lately, Elizabeth Rosetta. Catherine didn't understand where the name Rosetta had come from.

Susanna's behaviour had worsened since Catherine moved into John Cawley's house in Hobart, but John was another layer of security. Catherine struggled with her wages as a servant. James Blay Jr, Susanna's father, made no contact nor contributed financially. The Post Master told her that a captain who sailed many trips between Hobart and Adelaide, said James Jr had married a woman called Sarah Broadbent. He'd started another family. She wondered if the law would catch up with him—they were still married.

John Cawley suggested she sell the flour mill in Liverpool Street and they move to Longford, near Launceston. Apart from the year she spent in Adelaide she hadn't strayed from New Norfolk or Hobart. It could be time for a change. Susanna might benefit from a different location. The girl had become more obsessed with the scars on her fingers from putting her hands in the fireplace in Adelaide when she was an infant. No one else noticed them, but Susanna spent thirty minutes before bed every evening, rubbing pork fat into the ends of her fingers. Longford could have her focussing on a different life.

The decision made to move, Catherine put the flour mill in Liverpool Street up for sale. It had been twenty-four years since Teddy's passing. She needed a new life. Taking time aside from packing their belongings, Catherine asked John to write a letter to Margaret.

Dear Margaret, William and children

I trust you are all well and that the farm is still thriving as it was last time you wrote. I have met a lovely man John Cawley (who is writing this for me) and with Susanna, we are moving to Longford, near Launceston.

Susanna's behaviour is worrying, she refuses to attend school, and obsesses over the scars on the ends of her fingers from the fire in Adelaide. John and I think a change will be good for her. We will write with our new address once we are settled.

Love to you all,
Mother

18

MARGARET

Charity
"Charity was a traditional Christian virtue and all churches
supported parishioners suffering misfortune and reached out to
other flocks (even 'heathens') with benevolence, tinged with moral
fervour and missionary zeal, to bring them into the fold."

https://dictionaryofsydney.org/entry/health_and_welfare

"However, in those boom years Melbourne's death rate from typhoid
was in fact worse than London's and diphtheria was almost as bad."

*http://collingwoodhs.org.au/wp-content/uploads/3-Early-Collingwood-
Memories-In-Those-Days.pdf*

Collingwood, Melbourne, 1848

Margaret opened the letter from her sister-in-law, hoping
Elizabeth had good news to share. Margaret's own life was in
disarray. She was with child again, and John Douglas was still sickly.

Terror gripped her heart every time John sneezed or coughed; they couldn't afford a doctor. William was not working, and his melancholia permeated every facet of their lives. She'd taken in mending to earn enough money to feed the children. Adding another to the mix was a pressure she didn't look forward to.

Gawler Street, Portland

Dear Margaret

We are settled in a new, grand, house in Portland, and the farm is doing well. John is working hard.

I must share some surprising news, I am carrying twins, due later this year. The midwife said she can feel two heads, and I can see two heads sticking out of my belly. I am enormous and am finding it difficult to go about my normal duties. I thank God He gave me some time away from childbirth. Elizabeth is now five and will be able to help with the new infants. The other children are at school.

Are your children well? Are you? Is William settled in Collingwood?

Please write soon and let me know how you all are.

Love to you all,
Elizabeth

Kneeling next to the chair William sat in in the parlour all day, Margaret read Elizabeth's letter to him. 'Elizabeth is having twins, William. Isn't that amazing?' She hoped the happy news would cheer him. He looked at her, smiled, and turned his head back to the window.

On Sunday, after church, Margaret approached the Minister of St Peter's asking if the Church could afford funds to pay a midwife. Margaret didn't want to have this baby on her own as she did John Douglas, and she didn't want to put the burden on Sarah or Maggie. Familiar with William's condition and Margaret's plight, the Minister didn't hesitate.

Fourteen-year-old Sarah ran for the midwife early in the afternoon of 22nd April. The real start of winter was still weeks away, but this April day the wind whipped up the dirt from the streets and blew it into Sarah's eyes. Clouds the colour of her father's mood hung low on the horizon, threatening to spill their watery contents onto the town below. She pulled the coat that didn't fit anymore, in across her chest with one hand, and held onto her cap with the other.

Holding an umbrella over hers and the midwife's head while the midwife encouraged her pony to pull the buggy, it pleased Sarah not to be running home in the rain and mud.

Twelve-year-old Maggie had the look of a terrified baby bird when Sarah and the midwife walked into Margaret's bedroom. Nine-year-old Caroline was supervising the younger children, while William sat in his chair in the parlour, looking out the window into the street.

Maggie had water boiling in the kitchen and clean towels underneath her mother. In the final throes of labour, Margaret smiled at her daughters. 'Thank you girls. I would be all at sea without you.'

Frances Amy Blay made her way into the world ten minutes after the midwife arrived. Margaret had calmed knowing her daughters wouldn't be alone as they were with the birth of John Douglas. This infant had a robust cry and a good colour. The midwife pronounced her as fit and healthy.

William didn't leave his seat in the parlour.

'That's a lovely name, Mama,' Sarah said. 'Who is she named after?'

'No one, Sarah. I read the names in the birth section of the news-paper and liked them.'

'What if Papa doesn't like the baby's names?'

'I'm not inclined to be concerned about what your Papa will like, Sarah.'

19

WILLIAM

November 1848

I know it's hard for Margaret. I know that Sarah is taking on a lot of responsibilities to help her mother. But I find I can't become involved in life. I have failed. The only thing I enjoy doing is farming, and I've lost them both—Stoney Bank and Greenhills.

My farm in New Norfolk, Stoney Bank, was a delight, that is until the wool prices dropped in London and an economic depression hit Van Diemen's Land, dragging me along in its wake. Selling that farm for less than its value was heart-breaking. It meant we had the chance of a new start, but I can never return to Van Diemen's Land.

I have lost Greenhills and I will never earn enough money, ever again to have my own farm. I can't work at labouring because my leg aches from the moment I put my foot on the floor in the morning, until the moment I lift my leg onto the bed at night.

Could I take the family to Portland to be with my brother and his wife? Possibly. But what work could I do? I can't walk behind a plough. I can ride a horse, but what good is that? I can muck out stables and feed animals and collect eggs—women's work – I won't do that on my brother's farm.

So I sit here all day and look out the window. I know I am getting worse; I know the level of care I need frustrates Margaret. I know my older children, Sarah and Maggie, have run out of patience with me. But I cannot bring myself to exist in their world.

The only way I can get out of bed in the morning is to live in my own world, one where I focus on the window.

"17 November 1848

Margaret Blay

Solicits the admittance of William Blay into the Lunatic Asylum."
1

"...Also it took just two signatures for somebody to be taken in. If a man wanted his wife gone, and his friends knew about it, he could get them to say his wife was mad, and she'd be taken.

"At one stage it also took two signatures to be discharged, but that was later increased to eight signatures, meaning it was a lot harder to get out."
2

"The humble petition of Margaret Blay of Collingwood in the city of Melbourne to his Honour C J La Trobe, Esquire Superintendent of Port Phillip.

Herewith:

That the husband of your petitioner, William Blay, was formerly a farmer on the River Plenty, and in prosperous circumstances. That between two and three years time it pleased Almighty God to afflict him by taking away his reason. That the consequence was that their former means of subsistence was suddenly and completely taken away, and your Petitioner has, with the assistance of charitable friends struggled to support her husband and family by needlework.

That the precarious nature of such a means of livelihood has placed them in a state of constant distress, and together with the charge of their family of seven children, all under 14 years of age, has prevented your Petitioner from paying that attention to her husband which he much requires. That latterly, your Petitioner's husband has become not only unable to take care of himself in any degree, but is now almost entirely beyond his reason, and that her case has become one of such distress as to cause her well nigh to sink below the limits. Her circumstances are well known to the priest D Newham, the Minister of St Peter's Church, who would willingly bear witness to the correctness of these statements, and her truly melancholy position.

She therefore humbly begs your Honour to exercise your kindness towards herself and her family by placing her afflicted husband in the Lunatic Asylum near Melbourne, and your Petitioner will ever feel the greatest gratitude.

Signed: Margaret Blay

Collingwood, 16th November 1848

I sanction this application

Signed: William a'Beckett

Resident Judge." [3]

"I certify that I have known William Blay to be afflicted with insanity for upwards of two years. I further certify that I have this day examined him and find his case more aggravated. I am therefore of opinion that he is a fit person to be as soon as possible put under proper treatment in a Lunatic Asylum

Signed: Wm Fleming, Surgeon

Melbourne, November 13 1848

I hereby certify that I have examined Wm Blay and find he is of unsound mind.

Signed: P. Cu? M.D.

November 14th 1848." [4]

20

MARGARET

Collingwood, November 1848

M argaret told the doctor how old her children were while he
wrote the letter to have William admitted to the insane
asylum. Unable to cope with her husband's deteriorating mental
state, Margaret took advice from friends at church and began the
proceedings to have her husband taken away.

He didn't resist when they came to collect him. He didn't
acknowledge he was being removed from their home. Margaret
kissed his forehead as two attendants took William under the arms
and lifted him out of his chair. His refusal, or his inability to walk,
Margaret wasn't sure which, meant he was placed on a hospital
stretcher and taken outside to the transport. The neighbours gath-
ered to peer and gossip. Margaret closed the door behind the hospital
attendants, not waiting to see if her husband turned to acknowledge
her. Turning back into the hallway, she noticed seven-year-old Elizabeth standing at the other end.

'Where are those men taking Papa?' she asked.

The children were supposed to be in the kitchen where Margaret had instructed Sarah to keep them. She could hear Frances crying. The infant would be wailing for a feed.

'Go back into the kitchen and help your sisters with the boys and the baby. I'll explain in a minute.'

Elizabeth stood her ground. 'I want to know where Papa has gone.'

Margaret walked towards the child, took her hand and led her back into the kitchen. She would keep it simple and brief, the same explanation would have to suffice for them all.

'Papa has gone to hospital,' she began, 'he has not been well. You know he sits in his chair in the parlour all day and sometimes stays in bed. This can't go on, he needs doctors to take care of him. Some people from the hospital came and helped Papa into their wagon. They have taken him to see if they can make him better.'

There were no tears to wipe from her eyes. There was no flood of relief to lift the weight of the last three years from her shoulders. The body of her husband had been taken away; but his mind, spirit, and person, had left long ago.

'How long will he be away?' Sarah asked.

'Until he is better,' Margaret answered curtly. 'We have meals to prepare and chores to do. We will say a prayer for Papa at church on Sunday.'

21

WILLIAM

The Yarra Bend Insane Asylum
"The straitjacket is described as early as 1772, in a book by the Irish physician David Macbride, though there are claims an upholsterer named Guilleret invented it in 1790 France for Bicêtre Hospital.
Before the development of psychiatric medications and talking therapy, doctors did not know how to treat mental disorders such as schizophrenia, depression, and anxiety disorders. They attempted treatments that are cruel by modern standards, and the straitjacket was one of them. At the height of its use, doctors considered it more humane than restraints of ropes or chains. It prevented the sufferer from damaging clothes or furniture, and from injuring self, staff, or fellow inmates"

https://en.wikipedia.org/wiki/Straitjacket

"Medical experiments akin to torture
By the 19th and 20th centuries, the western world had accepted that mental disorders were akin to medical illnesses.
This led to attempts to remedy mental illness using medical experiments that might now be described as torture.

Some particularly bizarre methods, described by Professor Scull, were designed to give people near-death experiences.

It was noticed that there were old stories dating back even to Roman times of people who had been shipwrecked, nearly drowned, and as a result of nearly drowning had recovered their wits — these were people who had previously been mad...

This hypothesis led to mental patients being put in cages and lowered into water.

The idea was that manipulating the patient's environment and providing a safe and forgiving place for them to be, could help restore them to sanity.

Within asylums, experimentation on a very vulnerable population continued, with little supervision.

"These kinds of interventions were made possible by the fact that the mad were seen as almost dead while alive"...

"They had lost all their rights. Madness was such a desperate condition, that any kind of desperate remedy could be tried." "

www.abc.net.au/news/health/2016-08-02/mental-illness-and-insanity-a-short-cultural-history/7677906

YARRA BEND PATIENT, IN THE BAG.

An 1862 illustration by Charles Frederick Somerton showing a Yarra Bend patient in a restrictive bag.

Picture: State Library of Victoria

November 1848

I knew there wasn't any point struggling with the large men who put their hands under my armpits and lifted me up out of my chair. When the doctor came the other day, I heard he and Margaret talking. Because I don't make a fuss and either do as Margaret tells me or sit or lay and let her take care of me, she thinks I am stupid and don't understand what is going on. I understand. I find I am incapable of joining in with conversations and am content to listen. I hear the children playing, fighting, learning; they are sounds I enjoy.

As these men carried me to the wagon parked at the front of our house, I turned my head to see if Margaret would bid me farewell. She wasn't there. The door was closed.

Although I didn't object to their handling of me, nor did I struggle to get out of their grasp, they strapped me into a cocoon like garment from head to toe. They left me like that for a long time. I don't know how long, there were no clocks and they took my watch. No one came back to see me once they'd thrown me on the bed in the cell. I wet myself because there was no way of release from the cocoon.

The cell they put me in, and I'll call it a cell, because it feels like a prison, has a window high up that I couldn't see out of even if I could stand up. I think of my Papa when he was on the prison hulk *Retribution* on the River Thames. That makes me sad. I'm on the bed, the only piece of furniture in the room. There is nowhere else to sit. Not even a table and a chair. I wondered about food. Would I eat in here? Or do they have a dining room? Will I get a chance to speak to someone? Anyone?

I lay on the bed until the last of the day's light filtered through that high up window. I wet myself three times, I think. I lost track. Thirsty and hungry, and wet, I called and called for hours. No one came.

This cell must face west. The morning light is weak. I wriggled so my head was down the other end of the bed. That way I could see the little bit of daylight that teased me through the gap just below the ceiling.

I don't know how long I've been in this place. Sometimes I see the morning sun, sometimes I don't. They've broken my spirit. Margaret and the children have not been to see me. I've asked, twice. The two times I asked they put me in a tranquiliser chair, poured cold water on my head and hot water on my feet. I didn't ask again. I've learned it's best to be compliant and do everything they say. If I obey, I don't get beaten. They leave me alone to sit in my room and stare at the wall. I get to eat in the dining room with other people, but the food isn't worth waiting for. I must eat it though, otherwise I get none the next day. I've learned that lesson.

Still, I miss Margaret and my children. Christmas has been and gone. I heard nurses talking about it being one of the hottest Christmases they could remember. I don't know how long ago that was now.

9 February 1849

I opened my eyes this morning, well I think it was morning, there was a light shining in the cell. But I didn't know where it came from. Mama was sitting on the bed holding my hand, and Papa was at the end of the bed, smiling. He told me everything would be all right and that I should let go and follow him and Mama.

22

MARGARET

February 1849

S arah looked after the small children while Margaret caught up on mending for customers. Apart from donations from the Church, this was her only income and the only way she could feed the children and pay the rent. Caroline and Elizabeth were at school. Doubting she would have enough money to send William, John or Frances to school when they were of the age, she planned to use the techniques her wonderful grandmother Sarah Blay had used when teaching her and Sadie. Her step-father James Blay Jr refused to let her and her sister attend school, but her resourceful mother found a way.

It felt awkward sitting in the chair William sat in for almost a year. But the light in the parlour was better than anywhere else in the house. She also had a good view of the street and could see her neighbours going about their business. A police officer in his crisp uniform walked past the window. Dread crept up Margaret's back and down her arms. Her mouth dried up. She knew the police officer would knock on her door, but it startled her when he did.

The officer took off his hat when she answered the door. 'Mrs

Blay?' he said, Margaret nodded. 'I have an urgent letter for you from the Yarra Bend Insane Asylum.' He held the letter toward her, but her hand wouldn't obey her brain's instructions to reach up and take it. 'Is there someone at home to help you?' the officer asked. Shaking her head, *no*, Margaret's hand followed her instructions and moved up to take the letter. Putting his hat back on, he gave a slight bow, and walked away from Margaret's door. She closed it.

The noise of children playing in the back garden reassured her they didn't know someone had come to the door. Pulling the parlour door closed behind her, Margaret sat in the armchair and opened the letter.

Dear Mrs Blay

I regret to inform you that your husband, William Blay, died in this Asylum on 9th February inst.

Please contact us regarding the burial requirements for your husband. If you cannot afford a burial, he will be placed in the cemetery of the grounds of the Asylum in an unmarked grave.

From: Public Records Office Victoria:
VPRS 7416/P1 Unit 1 - General Register of Admissions and Discharges (1848 - 1856) contained: General Register of male patients received and discharged from the Lunatic Asylum Melbourne
No. 10
William Blay
Age: 33 (sic) – (*would have been 40*)
No. in admission register: - 21
When Admitted: 25 Nov 1848
Whence: Melbourne
By what authority: His Honour C. J. La Trobe
Form of insanity: monomania
Discharged:9 Feb 1949

Cause of discharge: died
Remarks: none.

"William Blay was admitted to the asylum on the 25th Nov 1848 by his Honour C.J. La Trobe, at the request of his wife Margaret. Approximately 10 weeks later, on the 9 of Feb 1849 William Blay died in the asylum." [1]

23

ELIZABETH BLAY

"The flat ground of Collingwood was notorious for its flooding:
Within an hour, I have seen the results of a thunderstorm covering
two square miles of the Flat. Some have suggested mermaids
swimming about. I never saw one. They would have around in the
mud. Slippery, miry, and puddle all the winter, and caked with rough
clay in the summer, the difficulties of peregrination around
Melbourne after the influx of population in the early fifties were at
their worst on Collingwood Flat..."

*http://collingwoodhs.org.au/wp-content/uploads/3-Early-Collingwood-
Memories-In-Those-Days.pdf*

1850

I held on to my eldest sister, Sarah, I could not stop the flood of
tears. It was relentless. Mama told us over supper that Caroline,
William and I would no longer be going to the church school because
we were moving from Collingwood to Fitzroy. I am happy to be
leaving Collingwood when it rains the streets flood and you can't
leave the house without wellington boots on. I have none, Mama

can't afford to buy me a pair. But I love the learning being with other children, and I love my teacher. Mama says she doesn't have the money to find a new school in Fitzroy. I told her I could walk from the house in Fitzroy to school in Collingwood. She said no. It isn't fair. Mama works hard with lots of mending that people bring to the house, but she still hasn't got enough money. Sometimes I get furious with Papa. I think he is still in the hospital, but Mama has said nothing. She doesn't go to visit him or take us. I asked her once, and she said there were too many of us and Papa would get confused.

Sarah said she would help Caroline and me keep up with our reading and writing, but she is sixteen and will soon get married. She is already being courted by someone; I don't remember his name. I don't like him. Anyway, Mama needs her to keep the house and look after John and Frances, so she won't have time to teach us. Maggie wants to be a teacher and is fourteen, she doesn't have a boy knocking on the door to take her out, so Mama said Maggie should teach Caroline, me, and William. But I still want to go to school. I will miss school.

Mama said Papa taught her and our Aunt Sadie to read and write and work out numbers when Mama was a little girl. Her Papa wouldn't let her go to school. Why would he not let her go to school? Mama showed Maggie the way our Papa taught her to read hard words and write with ink. Maggie is showing us. I still miss school, but Maggie is trying very hard and even has our brother, William, who is a very, very, naughty boy, sitting down writing things in his books. He doesn't sit for long. When he is tired of the work, he runs outside and annoys the chickens and the goat. Mama says she will send him to work soon. She will find an apprenticeship for him. He is twelve, Mama says he is old enough.

It doesn't take us long to do our school work now, because Maggie doesn't have to worry about William. Mama found him an apprenticeship as a saddler. She said our cousin in Portland is a saddler, and his name is William too. I don't' remember our cousins. I was a baby when they moved away to Portland. I don't even know where that is.

Caroline and I work hard, and Mama has asked Maggie to teach

John Douglas how to read and write. He is almost six, so he is old enough. When we finish our lessons, Caroline and I help Mama with the sewing and the mending for her customers. Sarah looks after the house and the baby, Frances Amy. The baby is between two and three years and runs everywhere. She keeps Sarah busy. Maggie helps with the cooking when our lessons finish.

24

CATHERINE

Tasmania 1854

Catherine's hand shook as she put her mark on the permission paper for Susanna's marriage to Edward Lovell Dwyer. The child was fourteen and he, still a convict, was thirty. Her mother's remonstrations would not sway the girl. Susanna said his age didn't matter and the fact he was still a convict, didn't matter. She reminded Catherine that her first husband, James Tedder, was also a convict when she married him.

Susanna's father, James Blay Jr, had not seen his daughter since Catherine left Adelaide in 1839. The child had always been wild and headstrong, and if her mother's permission was not granted, she would live in the stable with Edward at his assigned labour.

Catherine and her friend John Cawley were the only witnesses to the wedding. Neither Edward nor Susanna had a circle of friends. Sadie, Catherine's second daughter, refused to attend. She told her mother that her indulgence of Susanna had led to the child's unruly behaviour and reckless lifestyle.

John had written to Margaret on Catherine's behalf, asking her to come to the wedding, but Margaret, with six-year-old Frances and eight-year-old, John, couldn't afford it. The wedding was a quiet affair.

25

ELIZABETH

Note: Susanna calls herself "Elizabeth" on her marriage certificate.[1]

George Street, Fitzroy 1855

Sarah was in her bedroom, the one she shared with Maggie, sitting on the side of the bed with her head in her hands. Her body was moving up and down although she wasn't making a noise. I knew she was crying. When I asked her what was wrong, she told me to ask Mama.

That night at supper, I asked Mama why Sarah had been crying. Mama's face screwed up and her lips looked as if they were stuck together. Her eyebrows disappeared under her hair when she pulled the face. She looked at Sarah and shook her head.

'You are all old enough to know. Frances Amy isn't but she won't understand. Sarah has been asked by her beau, Thomas Rowley Briggs, to marry him.'

I squealed, I was so excited 'That's wonderful, Sarah. That's happy news. Why were you crying about it?'

'I wasn't crying about it, Elizabeth, I was crying because I asked Mama if Papa could come out of the hospital to go to the wedding, and she told me Papa died six years ago.' Sarah got up from the table and ran to her room. I followed her.

Sarah threw herself on the bed and cried so hard and loud I thought the neighbours would come in to see what was happening.

'Why didn't Mama tell us when Papa died?' I asked Sarah. 'We've been thinking he's alive all this time. Poor Papa.' I lay on the bed next to my sister and hugged her until she stopped sobbing.

Sarah wasn't happy with Mama. She hardly spoke to her. Even on the day of her wedding to Thomas Rowley Briggs, Sarah didn't hug Mama. After their wedding, Sarah and Thomas went back to his house. Sarah gave Maggie, Caroline, me, Frances, and our brothers a hug, but she pecked Mama on the cheek without embracing her. When Sarah closed the door behind her, tears were running down Mama's cheeks.

1856

A letter came today, the postman brought it to the door. It was addressed to Mama, I put it on her sewing table in the parlour. We rarely got letters, so it was exciting to wonder about its contents. Mama was delivering some clothes she'd mended for the police officer's wife. She would stay there for a cup of tea, so I had to wait even longer to find out who the letter was from and what it was about.

'Mama, Mama, there is a letter for you, I put it in the parlour,' I called out to my mother when I heard her come in the front door. She didn't answer. Running up to the parlour I saw Mama had the letter open, she had a big smile on her face. She hadn't looked that happy... I couldn't remember the last time I saw my mother smile.

'It is good news,' she said. 'Sarah has had a baby girl. Her name is

Isabella Jane. My first grandchild. I'll have to write to your Grand-mama to tell her she is a Great Grandmama.' The smile disappeared from Mama's face after she finished telling me the good news.

'What else does it say, Mama?'

'Sarah and Thomas are moving to New South Wales. They will call in to see us on their way through.'

The joy at hearing the news of the new baby quickly disappeared as I realised I probably wouldn't see my sister Sarah, again. New South Wales was a long way.

26

ELIZABETH BLAY

Lake Tyers, Gippsland

"Lake Tyers Mission Station was established in 1861 by the Church of England missionary, John Bulmer. It was situated on Lake Tyers in Gippsland and accommodated local Aboriginal people and others who were moved there from reserves such as Coranderrk, Ebenezer and Ramahyuck when they closed. In 1971 the Victorian Government returned the land to the Aboriginal community. It is now known as Bung Yarnda.

In May 1863 the Victorian Government gazetted an area of 2,000 acres as the Lake Tyers Reserve. It was increased to 4,000 acres. This included 16 acres under cultivation, an orchard and stock. John Bulmer managed the Reserve until his resignation at the end of 1907. The Government took over in 1908 and restricted the residents' freedom of movement and narrowed the school curriculum. The buildings, which numbered 17, included a church and school room. The daily routine for the population included religious services twice a day, while the children had daily bible classes.

Unlike the managers of other Reserves, Bulmer had encouraged the residents to maintain their culture and their hunting practices as a means of supplementing their rations.

In 1906 the residents from Ramahyuck moved to Lake Tyers, followed by others from Lake Condah and Coranderrk, when they closed.

In 1917 the Central Board for the Protection of Aborigines adopted a policy of 'concentrating' all Aboriginal people at the Lake Tyers Station.

The residents, with the support of Pastor Doug Nichols and the Aborigines Advancement League, resisted Government assimilation policies. Between 1956 and 1965 they agitated for the Station to become an independent, Aboriginal-run farming cooperative. In 1965 it was declared a permanent reserve."

https://www.findandconnect.gov.au/ref/vic/biogs/E000928b.htm [1]

George Street, Fitzroy. 4 January 1862

My heart was all a flutter. I met a gentleman at my sister Caroline's wedding to her sweetheart, John Bulmer. He was a friend of John's. I wanted to scold Caroline for keeping him from me.

'He is tall, distinguished, with a dashing moustache and sky-blue eyes,' I told my fourteen-year-old sister Frances after Caroline's wedding. 'He hails from Belfast, he arrived here in 1855 and told me all about his father's drapery business in Belfast. His brothers have set up a branch of the family business in Nelson, in New Zealand. Imagine that, Frances. He has travelled all the way from Belfast to Melbourne and now has plans to go to New Zealand. I've never left Melbourne.'

'I've never left Melbourne either,' Frances complained.

'Yes, but you are a fourteen-year-old girl, Frances. I am a woman. He will come calling next week.'

. . .

I sat in front of the dressing table in the bedroom I shared with Frances and made sure every strand of hair was in place, and that I hadn't used too much rouge on my cheeks. Standing up, I straightened my dress and slipped my feet into my shoes.

'How do I look?' I asked Frances.

'You look beautiful, Elizabeth. He will fall in love with you.'

I felt my face go red at Frances' comment. I hoped David liked the way I looked. Frances plopped my sun hat on my head, and I left the straps to tie in place later. We went into the parlour to wait for David to come calling.

Introducing David to Mama was awkward. He was the first man I'd kept company with and watching my mother look him up and down made me feel uncomfortable. David didn't seem to notice.

After asking Mama what time I should be home, he put my arm in his, and led me outside to a waiting carriage. Never having had the experience of being picked up at the front door by a carriage, I expected it to have other people sitting inside.

'Is it just us in the carriage?' I asked David.

'Dear,' he said. 'My housekeeper has packed us a picnic lunch, and we will enjoy it at the Botanic Gardens. Do you find that agreeable?'

'Oh, yes, David,' I blurted. 'I have been waiting impatiently for this day to come.'

Wednesday 2 July 1862

Frances helped me into my wedding dress and Maggie fixed my hair. The dress flowed onto the floor. It had hoops half way down the dress —three of them - and ruffles. Frances touched it at every opportunity. It had long sleeves, with ruffles at the cuffs, and ruffles at the dipped neckline. I didn't wear a veil, instead I wore a delicate white cap which Maggie helped clip to my hair.

Frances asked me how much I thought the wedding dress cost.

'I don't know. I thought it rude to ask, it was very generous of David to buy it for me, don't you think?'

'Oh, yes, Elizabeth. You are so lucky to have found such a man.'

'At least he has sustained his success, not like Papa,' I mumbled when Frances moved away to pick up the flowers.

'Your dress is beautiful, too, Frances. You look beautiful. One of David's brothers or friends might take a liking to you at the wedding.'

'I will be too busy being a bridesmaid to look at men,' Frances blushed. 'Have you asked Mama about your wedding night?' The colour on her cheeks intensified, she turned purple. Maggie growled at her for her rudeness. I wondered if Maggie would ever get married. She was the second eldest and Sarah, Caroline and now me, were married. Maggie didn't have any men come calling.

'I'm not asking Mama about my wedding night,' I told Frances. 'When David proposed I wrote to Sarah Susanna. She has had three children already. She told me what to expect but said how much pain our first experiences caused me would depend on how gentle David is. I don't want to talk about it anymore else I will worry. I want to enjoy the wedding. What comes after will happen as it will.'

"McBeth (sic)-Blay – On the 2 ult at the residence of the bride's mother, George Street, Fitzroy, by the Rev. James Ballantyne, of Erskine Church, Carlton, Mr David Francis, youngest son of the late Mr George McBeth, of Cavan, t Elizabeth, fourth daughter of the late Mr. William Blay, formerly of Stony (sic) Bank Farm, New Norfolk, Tasmania, and late of Greenhills Station, Plenty River, Victoria." [2]

David was as gentle and caring as I could have hoped. He told me he understood I would have discomfort and pain but said that would pass and he hoped I would come to enjoy our sexual relationship. When he undid the straps at the back of my wedding dress, I stepped out with care, not wanting to stand on it. When he slipped the petticoat straps from my shoulders, my skin tingled, goose bumps ran up and down my arms. He kissed my neck. I wondered if this was his first time but thought it best not to ask. Undoing the corset that held up my breasts, his fingers ran down my back and across to my bare bosom. My nipples became erect and the goose bumps travelled from my arms to my breasts and down to between my legs. I shuffled my feet to temper the warm throbbing that pulsed in my private parts. David held my shoulders and turned me to face him. As I stood in my stockings and shoes, he unbuttoned his shirt, let it slip on the floor, undid his pants and stepped out of them. He grinned. Pulling me close, he pushed my legs apart and tickled my private parts with his fingers. The throbbing increased to so much I thought I would scream. Sarah Susanna didn't tell me any of this. Leading me to the bed, David told me to sit on the edge while he took off my shoes, and removed my stockings, his fingers kept up the tease. Yes, it was uncomfortable at first, but the experience was nothing I expected, and I couldn't wait for the next time.

Although I didn't find it to my liking, I understood why David wanted to rent a house rather than buy one. He was saving to contribute to the family business in New Zealand. When we leave for Nelson, he doesn't want the worry of selling a house in Melbourne. Renting also gives me the opportunity to be near Mama and Frances. Mama will help with the baby.

David doesn't understand how important it is to me that he is stable and has a sensible approach to money. He didn't live in Melbourne, or Collingwood when lots of people were poor, including our family. He arrived during the Gold Rush and to him, Melbourne appeared awash with money. Especially because he got a job straight away.

I haven't told him about Papa's poor choices. I haven't told him that some weeks if the Church didn't give Mama money, we wouldn't have had enough to eat. I haven't told him that Caroline, and I had to leave school because Mama couldn't afford to send us, and that she needed us at home to help with the sewing and mending she took in. I don't want him to feel sorry for us.

David earns a good income and for the first time in my memory I can eat when I feel like it and buy the clothes I want and need. His drapery expertise means I am dressed in the latest fashions. David knows Papa died in hospital, but he doesn't know big, strong, men came and took him away.

I am happy for Mama too. Her station in life has improved. There is even a new man in her life, Joseph McGinty[3]. When the time comes for David and I move to New Zealand, I know Mama will be comfortable. It's fortunate that my brother William James is infatuated with Elizabeth Jane Welch; he'll marry her and not be a bother to Mama any longer. I heard Mama telling Joseph that William James was too like Papa. My little baby brother, John Douglas followed Caroline and her husband John Bulmer, to Lake Tyers in Gippsland. He had the romantic idea that working on a mission station with the Aborigines would settle his agitated spirit. Mama says John inherited Papa's restless tendencies, and she doesn't think he will settle. Maggie is a teacher, and is yet unmarried, but she has a home of her own in Moray Place. Mama and Frances live at Maggie's house. I'm glad, they can all support each other. Frances wants to be a teacher too. I miss my eldest sister, Sarah Susanna. She looked after me and the boys when we were little. Sarah took on a lot more responsibility after they took Papa away. Mama put lots of pressure on Sarah. I hope Sarah is happy with Thomas.

Mine and David's first child came into the world less than a year after our marriage. We called her Elizabeth Nicholson McBeath. David's mother was Susan Nicholson. David explained that although he hailed from Belfast, the family originally came from Scotland. Elizabeth's name was part of the Scottish naming pattern. We will call her *Lizzie*.

David has repaid his loan to the Family Colonization Loan

Society[4] for his fare to Sydney and has been setting aside money to fund our move to New Zealand. Apparently he misses his brothers and looks forward to working with them in the family business in Nelson. I wonder if he thinks about how I will miss my mother and sisters when we leave.

27

MARGARET

Fitzroy, 1864

Margaret sat down on the end of her bed to read her mail. She'd received two letters today, one from her eldest daughter, Sarah, and one from her sister, Sadie. Sarah hadn't been back to Melbourne since she left for New South Wales with her husband not long after her first child, Isabella was born. Margaret had seen none of Sarah's other children, nor Isabella since she was a baby. It saddened her to think how she'd grown up in Hobart Town and New Norfolk, close to her Grandmama Elizabeth, and her step-grandparents, Sarah and James Blay. They had always been a part of each other's lives. Her mother's sisters and their husbands were on hand to help when needed, and her mother had assisted or delivered, Aunt Sophia's and Aunt Betsy's babies. Now she was alienated from her eldest daughter's life, hadn't seen her sister or mother for over twenty years, and her third daughter, Caroline was living 220 miles away with her missionary husband in Lake Tyers. Her youngest son, John Douglas lived in Lake Tyers too. Caroline wrote two or three times a year, and always included news about her brother, John.

Margaret and Elizabeth Blay, her brother-in-law John's wife, wrote to each other when they could. They had a close bond when they both lived in Melbourne before John took his family to Portland —220 miles away in the other direction from Lake Tyers - and before William borrowed money to buy 160 acres at River Plenty. Margaret kept all the letters in a small tin in her dressing-table drawer and took them out to read when she was lonely.

"Dear Mama

I hope this letter finds you well. Thomas and I and the children are well. I write to let you know that Thomas and I have a son. His name is Henry Thomas Briggs. Like you, Mama, after four girls I finally have a boy. However, I hope he is a better person than my brother, William James. I don't mean to cause you offence by that comment.

Isabella is now eight and doing very well at school, Amy Caroline started school this year. Annie Eliza, now four, and Elizabeth Mary who is just eighteen months are with me during the day. We are fortunate that Thomas can afford a cook and housekeeper, like you had in New Norfolk with the convicts, but these are employees. With my five children and a husband and a house to manage, I understand the difficulties you faced, especially when Papa became ill.

Please write soon to let me know how things are in Melbourne.

With love,
Sarah"

Disappointed at the brevity of the letter, Margaret did notice that Sarah had softened toward her, and signed "with love". She would write back without delay, telling her that William James had married Elizabeth Jane Welch, and they had a son, William James Blay. She would tell Sarah that she hoped the marriage and the child would help William overcome his self-obsessed nature.

Her hands trembling, Margaret opened the letter from her sister. They wrote often to each other, but this letter sent Margaret's heart racing, she had a bad feeling about its contents.

"My dear sister,

With the wonderful advancement in transportation, my dear Felix tells me that you should have this letter one week after I send it. Just imagine that, Margaret! Seven days for news to travel from Hobart to Melbourne.

Next time you write to Caroline, please give her our congratulations on the birth of her first child, William. It is nice that she named him after her Papa.

I now begin by telling you about our daughters. Our dear Margaret moved home with Felix and I after her husband Henry Cameron died a few months after they married, in 1861. But you know that. She hasn't found anyone else and doesn't appear to be interested. She pines for happiness but won't go and look for it. Sometimes I despair that she behaves the way you described your William before he passed away. Felix says I worry too much. Rosetta Kate is now fourteen and quite a cheerful, pleasant girl. Her schooling is finished, and Felix has found her employment in one of the shops in Hobart where they sell fancy dresses for the well to do ladies who want to look like they live in London. She seems to enjoy it. Marion Geraldine Lavinia attends school – as we were not allowed – and she can't wait to get there each morning.. Our girls are a joy, Margaret, I wish they had grown up knowing you.
Now to the part of my letter I have avoided facing. Mama is quite

*unwell. She is living with us in Hobart and is no longer with her
friend John Cawley. He disappeared when she became sick. Our
half-sister, Susanna, who now has two children, a boy, Edward
Sydney Dwyer, who is almost nine years, and a girl Rosetta
Phillipa who was born in 1860, told Mama to go back to Hobart
when John left. To my surprise Susanna is still with Edward Lovell
Dwyer, but it remains to be seen if that is forever. So, Mama is
living with Felix and me and the girls. The doctor does not know
what is wrong with her, but she is becoming very thin and can no
longer work as a servant. Felix is supporting her financially.
Mama is too unwell to travel to see you. Are you able to come home
to Tasmania for a visit?*

I look forward to all your news

With love, your sister, Sadie"

Margaret refolded Sadie's letter and put it in the tin with the others.
Right at the back of the drawer was another tin with money she had
been putting aside for many years. Counting, it, she knew she had
enough to visit her sister and mother in Tasmania.

28

ELIZABETH BLAY (NEE FOGARTY)

Portland, Victoria, 1862

At forty-six years of age, Elizabeth Blay gave birth to a son. Stillborn, her husband John, ordered the child not have a name. They would register his birth and death as "unnamed". [1] After giving birth to fourteen children, two of whom had died, Elizabeth wanted to remember each of her children. She called the perfectly formed little boy *Fogarty* and would keep his memory and the picture of his beautiful, pink, flawless, face in her heart. When she called his memory to her mind, she would know he was *Fogarty*, not "unnamed".

Portland, 1865

My dear sister-in-law, Margaret. I am happy at the news that your daughter Elizabeth married her sweetheart, David Francis McBeath and that she is expecting her second child. Your letter has sung his praises. It is fortunate that your daughter married someone with a good trade and income.

It is with great sadness that I share with you two forms of tragic news. I gave birth two years ago to a perfectly formed, beautiful little boy who had already passed away before he left my body. You will know the heartache that follows such a birth, from your assistance in Melbourne at the birth of the daughter I lost. John decreed the child not be named, but I secretly called him Fogarty. I call this name to mind when I want to remember him.

My second piece of tragic news is that my husband, John, has disappeared. The police are confident there is no foul play involved. He left the house one morning as usual, to work on the farm, and did not return for dinner or supper. My sons, James, William and John searched for him, as did many other people in the district. His horse and some few personal belongings are also missing. It seems he has deserted me and the children. The youngest, Harriet, is but nine years. I am fortunate that Elizabeth Comet has not yet married and is at home still. She has been a comfort and a support. What is the explanation for the behaviour of the men we married, Margaret? James Jr deserted your mother, Catherine, William became mad, and now John has deserted me and his children. The older boys are running the farm and still earning money.
I will finish now as I am on the verge of tears and have a feeling of desperation eating into my heart.

Your loving sister-in-law, Elizabeth.

29

ELIZABETH

Childbirth

"Pain relief becomes acceptable, even fashionable
1847 — ether used by Scottish physician James Simpson to treat
labor pain
1853 — Queen Victoria uses it for birth of Prince Leopold, gives
Simpson a baronetcy in gratitude for the 'blessed chloroform' "

http://www.elenagreene.com/childbirth.html

Napier Street, Fitzroy. 17 April 1865

David has left for work. The pains of childbirth have started.
Lizzie is grizzling and won't settle. I think she is getting teeth. I
call out to my youngest sister, Frances. Mama suggested she stay with
us as the end of my confinement grew near. I'm glad I listened to her.

'My pains have started, Frances. Please get Mama. And hurry
back, Lizzie will need your attention.'

My youngest sister is an intelligent, easy-going young woman.
She's seventeen in a few days and doesn't seem to have any interest in

finding a husband. She says she will start her own school, right here in Melbourne.

Even though winter is still weeks away, it's cloudy and grey outside. I remind Frances to put on her coat before she leaves the house. Lizzie was born on a lovely, sunny day. This baby is coming into the world on a day with a grey, dismal outlook and the continuing threat of rain. I hold my stomach and pray the weather isn't an omen.

Mama puts towels on the bed and has me lay down. The pains are closer together and stronger. She puts Lizzie in her crib and tells Frances to get the doctor. I drown Lizzie's cries of indignation at suddenly being put back in her crib, with my screams. This baby is determined to come into the world as soon as possible.

When the doctor arrives I feel as if the infant is dragging my insides out with it. He puts a mask over my nose and mouth and tells me to breathe. Although I am awake, the wrenching pain subsides.

'It's a boy,' the doctor announces as he cuts the cord. With his work done, the doctor hands my son to the midwife who cleans him and wraps him in a blanket. 'I want to see him,' I say. She hands my son to me while I gather my thoughts and wonder how long it will be before my body recovers from the trauma of this birth.

Mama is smiling. 'He is a big boy,' she says. 'Big and strong, David will be happy.'

I nod. A smile I can't stop from appearing, spreads across my face. 'Yes, David will be elated.'

'What will you name him?' Mama asks.

'I'll wait until David sees him. He will decide.'

David must have heard the baby's cries as he opened the front door. He came rushing into the bedroom, almost slipping on the hallway rug. Mama and the midwife had left, and Frances was tending to Lizzie. 'It's a boy,' I said to him before he had the chance to ask. I couldn't stand his look of apprehension. The grin on my husband's face spread from one side to the other. His eyes lit up so much they appeared to be reflecting the light coming through the windows.

'His name will be William after your father, and George after mine,' David said. He sat on the chair next to the bed and stroked the baby's dark head in time with the infant's suckling. 'He is a big boy, Elizabeth. Are you well?'

After assuring my husband I would recover with a few days' rest, he went into the kitchen to make us both a cup of tea. I could hear him humming, but I wasn't familiar with the tune. Perhaps it was from Northern Ireland or Scotland. Our son, William George McBeath went to sleep in my arms. I lay him on the bed next to me and slid down under the covers. We'd both had a busy day.

30

CATHERINE

Hobart, 11 July 1866

Wednesday. Catherine wasn't sure why it was important for her to know the day of the week. It didn't matter what the days were; she knew she didn't have long for this world. But each morning when the sun's rays found their way into her bedroom and danced on the bed, working their way up to her face, she asked her middle daughter Sadie, what day it was. The days all blended into each other, she wanted to keep track.

'It's a typical winter's morning, Mama,' Sadie said. 'The sun is shining but there is no warmth in its rays. The wind is howling and bringing with it the icy blast from the snow on Mt Wellington. You stay in bed, snug and warm.'

Margaret had sailed from Melbourne to visit. They hadn't seen each other for almost thirty years. Margaret's three older children, born in New Norfolk, were the only ones of Margaret's children Catherine had seen. A whole family had been born and grown up, and she hadn't been a part of it. Grateful to have been a part of Sadie's life, and to have been a grandmama to her three girls, Catherine asked Margaret to share news of her grandchildren and great-grandchildren.

Margaret pulled up a chair and sat on it by her mother's bed. When she picked up Catherine's hand Catherine wondered if she would notice that her veins were visible through the skin. Her bent fingers and swollen knuckles made her hands look like an old crone's. If she did notice, Margaret didn't indicate it. With her free hand, she stroked her mother's brow. Catherine listened to stories of her grandchildren and great grandchildren. There was no mention of having to explain a convict past. It seemed they had left the convict stain behind in Tasmania.

Catherine squeezed Margaret's hand and sent her for Sadie. With her two older daughters sitting either side of the bed, Catherine asked them to listen to her story.

'I loved your father more than life itself,' she began 'from the moment I saw him walking up from the Derwent, carrying his pack and anything else Papa had lumbered him with. His smile lit up the world. The sun's rays danced on his hair and kissed his fair, English skin. He was a man like no other I had seen. He didn't display the scars of punishment and transportation, although with the stories he told me when we lay in bed at night, I was amazed he survived with his sanity.

'He started the flour mill in Liverpool Street, so he could make enough money to take us to England to see his father, Henry, and his mother, Sarah. I humoured him in the dream, but I didn't want to go.

'My Papa really liked him. When I look back, I wonder if your Papa reminded your Grandpapa of himself. Your Papa, James was a hard worker, didn't get involved in petty arguments with others, and focussed on his family and work. The day each of you were born he hugged me, and between torrents of tears, thanked me for you. I thought we would be happy forever, the four of us. Although I did secretly hope and pray that I would one day be able to give him a son. He didn't worry about having daughters, he said he wouldn't care if we had seven, as long as we were all healthy and happy. My life broke into fragments of a thousand pieces the day he died. I knew I would never fully recover, and I didn't.

'I know you both wonder why I married James Blay Jr. While your Papa was alive, James made you shoes, visited regularly, and brought you both small treats. Your Papa didn't like him very much because of his business dealings. When your Papa died, James wrote to your grandparents in England for me, telling them about the tragedy. He looked after us in those first few months. He chopped wood for the fire, he mended gates and fences, and made you both more shoes. When he proposed, I was besotted with his generosity and kindness. And I was lonely.

'As you know, it didn't take long for his true colours to appear. He wanted your Papa's land and buildings to have as his own. You know the difficulties we had over the years. But there were times when he really did love me. He would show much affection and kindness to me and to the two of you. It was hard for me to resist him each time he came back for me.

'You were both angry when I took Susanna and went to Adelaide, I know. But at the time it felt right. It didn't take him long to drag his true self out from under the veil of decency. That last time I knew I would never return to him.

'I'm told he married in Adelaide, even though he is still legally married to me. He started a whole new family that Susanna will never know. I despair for her and her future, but she will not see me. When I die, please let her know I love her, and that I am sorry her father has neglected her.'

Both Margaret and Sadie admonished their mother for speaking of her death. Smiling at them both, she told them she loved them, and asked if they would get her a cup of tea and something to eat. Catherine listened to them chatting while they filled the kettle, she could hear china clinking and food being collected from the pantry.

As she turned her head to look out the window at the dreary July day, it filled with a purple and orange light. The love of her life, James Tedder, stepped through the light into the room, holding his arms out to her. He helped her out of bed, kissed her lips, and holding her hand, led her to the light in the window.

Margaret stayed for her mother's funeral, then sailed back to Melbourne. She hadn't told her mother about John Blay deserting Elizabeth.

31
_____

ELIZABETH

New Zealand.

"As New Zealand entered the final third of the 19th century the South Island dominated the economy, largely due to the impact of wool and gold. Canterbury lived literally on the 'sheep's back' to became the country's wealthiest province. The discovery of gold in central Otago in 1861 helped Dunedin become New Zealand's largest town. Thousands of young men rushed to New Zealand hoping to make their fortune as they followed the gold from Otago to the West Coast and later to Thames in the North Island. Few struck it rich on the goldfields but the collective value of the gold that was discovered kick-started the economy.

A young, mobile and male-dominated population was typical of many frontier societies. Provincial and central governments believed that the country's future growth and progress required the order and stability offered by family life. Various schemes were developed to attract women migrants and families to New Zealand in a bid to help society mature."

https://nzhistory.govt.nz/classroom/ncea3/19th-century-history-1870-1900

"The New Zealand wars were a result of disputes over land sovereignty between the British and colonial forces and Māori tribes. Around 2000 Australians enlisted for this conflict. Most came from Victoria, although a number of British troops stationed in Australia were sent to fight in New Zealand. British soldiers in a number of regiments based in Australia were also sent across the Tasman as a military force at various times between 1845 and 1847 and between 1860 and 1866."
https://guides.slv.vic.gov.au/colonialforces/newzealandwars

"In 1858 Nelson had:
17 merchants
25 storekeepers including 5 bakers, 5 butchers, 9 milliners, 4 breweries, 12 shoemakers, 4 blacksmiths, 17 carpenters, 9 cabinet makers, 6 boarding houses
434 wooden buildings
27 brick or stone buildings"
http://www.theprow.org.nz/events/nelson-becomes-a-city/#.W9E_ZfaYPbo

November 1866

I have never been far away from my mother, and today I pack up my clothes and my children's clothes to set sail on a ship across the Tasman Sea to New Zealand. David has been talking about going to New Zealand since we met, but until now, until today, it was an abstract concept. Now it is real. I will say goodbye to my mother and two of my sisters. Our family which has been through so much, is being even further fragmented.

We delayed our departure until William George was old enough to walk, and until David had reassurance from his brothers in New Zealand that the New Zealand Wars were finished. He told me we are going to the South Island, and the battles were on the North Island, but I was reluctant to go until he was certain.

I know Mama is desperately sad for us to leave. Lizzie and

William are the only two grandchildren she sees. My brother, William James has one surviving son, James Douglas, with his wife Elizabeth Jane Welch, but she is strange, and doesn't like William visiting his family. William James' son by the same name, died at less than one-year of age. I don't think my brother recovered from that loss.

David has ordered a buggy to take us to the port. We will say goodbye to Mama, Maggie and Frances here, in Fitzroy. The tears will be heartfelt and flow for a long time. David said it's best to get the crying done while we can hug each other and say goodbye.

I promise Mama I will come home to see her.

Lizzie is three years now, and she understands that something is happening. I told her we are going away for a while and she won't see her Grandmama until we can come back to visit. My little girl threw her arms around my mother's legs and said she didn't want to go. Mama picked the child up and hugged her until David prised Lizzie's arms away from her Grandmama's neck. Mama kissed William George who was holding my hand and trying to hide behind my skirts. He didn't understand what all the emotion was about.

'You be a good boy, and mind your Mama,' my mother said to William George. 'And you be good too, Lizzie,' she said as she straightened my daughter's hat and helped her into the buggy.

One more hug for each of them, and I turned and let David help me into the buggy. Lizzie sat by the window waving furiously until the vision of her aunts and grandmother was shrouded in dust. William George leaned in against his father, searching for the security he needed for a situation he didn't understand.

It took my breath away. The boat pulled into a beautiful harbour with water the colour of David's blue eyes. The sun's rays danced on the surface of the bay which reflected the trees that grew right down to the water's edge. No smells from drainage and sewage going into the streets, no northerly wind picking up the dust and throwing it into our faces and our hair. But the roads were as Collingwood was when we first moved there with Mama and Papa. I felt as if I'd sailed through a time warp and gone back twenty years.

The smile on David's face spread to his eyes, they sparkled and twinkled matching the water on the bay. Holding my hand as he helped me onto the dock, David leant in and kissed my cheek 'Isn't it beautiful?' he asked, handing William George to me.

'Yes, David, it's just lovely.' I said. 'Will your family come to meet us?'

He winked at me and said, 'I'll collect Lizzie, and we'll get some refreshments while we wait for our luggage and my brothers.'

Lizzie's hat had fallen and was dangling down the back of her neck. Her dress had stains from the orange she ate while waiting for the boat to tie up at the dock. She put her sticky, orange juice hand into mine and looked at me with the anticipation only a child can muster. 'Are we here, Mama?' she asked.

'Yes, Lizzie, we are here. Papa is organising our things and then getting us something to eat and drink. And we'll find a place to wash your face and hands.'

'I'm glad we are here, Mama. I don't think I would have been happy being on that awful boat for much longer.'

'Yes, we are all glad to be here, Lizzie,' I said.

Fifteen days on the Tasman Sea surrounded by sea sickness and bored children was enough. I couldn't imagine how trying it was for David travelling from Belfast to Sydney and then Melbourne.

David's brother, John, met us at the small establishment we had chosen for a drink and something to eat. He was shorter than David, but had the same sparkling blue eyes, and impeccable presentation. His Irish accent had a different inflection from David's, and after I'd heard a few people speak, I realised the accent here differed from ours in Melbourne. That was something I hadn't considered.

David and John had a brother, William who would meet us later. While the brothers were busy catching up and enjoying each other's company, Lizzie and William George's irritability grew. I hoped David would notice without me having to say anything. His brother did.

'The children and your wife are tired, David. Let's get them settled at my home. You and I can talk later.' John said.

The buggy David arranged, and which had our luggage stacked on the back, had waited for us outside the café. The horse stomped its front foot and waved its head up and down impatient to get moving. I knew how it felt.

John's home was timber and set back off the road, so the dust had somewhere to settle before it fell on the walls of the house, and the windows. There were three bedrooms, a kitchen, a parlour and a dining room. The six-roomed house was larger than anything we lived in in Collingwood or Fitzroy. I didn't remember the house at Greenhills, but Sarah used to lament the lack of space once we moved to Melbourne. She said the house at Greenhills was big, and there were only two children to a bedroom.

John graciously showed David and I to the guest bedroom and said William George and Lizzie could share the other. He said it didn't matter how long we took to find a place of our own, he would enjoy our company and getting to know me and the children. If I hadn't been so tired, I would have shown more excitement and gratitude. I thanked John and asked where I could bathe the children and get them ready for bed.

When David and I were finally alone and tucked up in a bed that didn't rock with the waves, he told me how happy he was to be with John. His brother, William, lived in Hokitika and would visit in a few days.

I lay awake for some time while David snored. He was pleased to be with his brothers and slept soundly knowing his plans were fulfilled. Whereas the sadness of leaving my mother and sisters so far away chipped at my heart until it found a place to hide.

32

MARGARET

Australian Rules Football

"Widespread leisure time on Saturday afternoons developed in Melbourne from the 1860s, well ahead of the rest of the world. It stemmed from the success of the building trades in winning the eight-hour day in 1856. Over the next decade, several trades negotiated deals of longer hours on weekdays for Saturday afternoons off."

"Immediate revisions occurred in July 1859; representatives of nine football clubs drafted The Victorian Football Rules in May 1860; and another full consolidation occurred in 1866.
But the most common reference is to a game on August 7 1858, commemorated in a statute at the Melbourne Cricket Ground. The first game of Australian football took place between elite schools Scotch College and Melbourne Grammar..."

"1860s and 70s
Within a few years of the drafting of the early rules, there were no

fewer than 19 football clubs using the rules drafted at the Parade Hotel."
https://theconversation.com/aussie-rules-rules-thanks-to-the-eight-hour-working-day-27630

Fitzroy, March 1867

The gas lights lit the streets of Melbourne and surrounding areas at night, so venturing out when the sun went down was safer and easier than it was when Margaret first moved back to Melbourne twenty years earlier. Her landlord, Joseph McGinty, had proven to be a considerate and caring gentleman and had taken an interest in her welfare. He often escorted her to outings on Saturday afternoons, or Sunday. This Saturday it was an evening outing, he was taking her to the theatre. She'd never been to the theatre and couldn't remember the last time she had looked forward to something with such excitement. Joseph had made his fortune during the Gold Rush and bought properties, one which Margaret rented.[1] He enjoyed the activities that came with plenty of disposable income. They were going to the Princess Theatre to see the Pride of Clarah. [2]

Margaret had made herself a new dress for the occasion and refashioned one of her old hats. She didn't own a coat that would be respectable enough to wear to the theatre and said a prayer of thanks when the March evening was mild, with no wind, and without the threat of rain.

Joseph picked her up in a horse and buggy, telling her how beautiful she looked. Trying not to blush like a child, Margaret let him help her into the buggy. The streets of Fitzroy and Melbourne were less dusty than when she and William first arrived in 1841, and when they returned in 1845. There were more people and the roads, used more frequently, had flattened and hardened. No need to be concerned about dust in her face, Margaret held onto her hat with one hand, and the edge of the buggy with the other. She was forty-eight and the feeling she had when she first realised how much she adored William when she was eleven, flooded into her heart. Shaking her head to clear it from any romantic notions, Margaret noticed Joseph looking at her. She blushed like a child and turned to watch the homes and businesses disappear as the buggy passed them.

When they arrived at the theatre, an attendant helped her out of the buggy and Joseph put her arm in his and led her into the foyer. Her shoes sunk into the carpet underfoot, the walls were adorned with pictures of actors and actresses, and waiters milled around the patrons holding trays with glasses of ginger beer for the ladies and beer for the men. Margaret felt like a princess. A bell rang, and Margaret, her arm in Joseph's accompanied him into the theatre where they were shown to their red, low backed seats. Although she didn't quite understand the play, Margaret enjoyed the music. The evening filled her with hope. A hope that her life might have turned a corner.

June 1867

Although it was a typical winter's day, Joseph's enthusiasm for the game of football he was taking her to, buoyed both their spirits. Joseph had bought her a new coat she was looking forward to wearing this afternoon. She'd heard talk of the game of football but had not seen it played. Joseph said they would play the match at Richmond Paddocks and the teams were Melbourne and Albert Park. Margaret didn't care who was playing, she was happy to be going out with Joseph, getting out of the house and away from her sewing.

Joseph hailed a coach and helped Margaret on board. She noticed he positioned himself near the window and realised when the coach moved up George Street that he was protecting her from the icy wind as it swirled in through every available space.

Standing in the cold wind, her coat buttoned up, her hat pulled down over her ears, Margaret couldn't keep herself from grinning.

She stood, on the edge of a playing field, watching men run around on a paddock kicking a ball, trying to prevent an opposition player from doing the same. It wasn't Margaret's preferred form of entertainment, but Joseph enjoyed the game, and she was with him.

33

ELIZABETH

Nelson, New Zealand September 1875

David's business is thriving, and he is happy in New Zealand. I have good company in his mother, Susan, who arrived six years ago from Belfast, and who lives with us, but I miss my mother and sisters.

Our seventh child, Ernest Douglas is a few weeks old and I worry about his health. He is a pasty colour and hasn't had a good appetite since birth. He is listless and limp, does not try to lift his head, and doesn't turn to follow anything that moves out of his line of sight. However, he has a beautiful little smile that lights up his whole face and make his blue eyes twinkle. He looks like David when he smiles. Our older children are well and healthy. Lizzie and William, born in Melbourne, are at school, as is Lilian Crosbie who was our first child born in Nelson, in 1868. Margaret Frances, born in 1870 will start school next year, at present she helps me with David Francis, born in 1871, Ethel born in 1874, and Ernest Douglas, the unwell baby. My husband says he isn't concerned about Ernest not thriving, he says he will improve when the weather does. I'm not convinced.

Wednesday 19 January 1876

The tap, tap on the front door was softer than expected from a caller. My mother-in-law answered it. She came into the kitchen where I was preparing breakfast for the children not attending school and said I should go to the parlour to see the visitor.

'Who is it?' I asked.

'A policeman. He won't tell me why he is here.'

My heart stopped. I could feel the last beat in my chest. I didn't feel it start again. I held my breath.

'Elizabeth, Elizabeth.' Susan called my name. 'Go to the parlour.'

My heart beat so fast I thought it would pop out of my chest. I put my hand over it as if that would help slow it down. The closer I got to the parlour door, the wilder my heart beat became.

The policeman stood in front of the fireplace, his hat under his arm. He stiffened when he saw me. 'Mrs McBeath, please sit down.' He offered me a seat in my own home. My heart raced at a frantic pace.

He didn't wait for me to ask why he was there. As soon as I sat down, he told me. David drowned in the Maitai River this morning. He went for a swim before work most mornings in the summer months as he had done this morning. The policeman said David's foot got caught on a snag in the water, and he couldn't free himself. He was 42. We'd been together only thirteen years.

We have seven children, the youngest is three months old. I can't get out of bed. Ernest Douglas is asleep in the bed with me. I feed him when he wakes, and then I put my head back on the pillow. David is dead. He isn't coming home. I don't know what we will do. I can't imagine living my life without him. His tenderness in our bed, his consideration of my needs, the way he hugged, loved, and played with our children. I will miss all that and more.

My brother-in-law John is organising David's funeral. His mother is looking after the children.

My eldest, thirteen-year-old Lizzie tiptoes into the bedroom and picks up Ernest to take him into the parlour. She kisses my forehead and touches my cheek with the back of her hand. I was seven when my father died but didn't find out until I was Lizzie's age. I didn't grieve or feel any sense of loss. Lizzie's eyes are red and swollen, the stains of hundreds of tears streak her face. She will miss her father.

Ernest is at home with my brother-in-law's housekeeper. She will watch him while the rest of us attend David's funeral. My other children stand by their father's graveside each displaying grief in their own way. The tears run down Lizzie's face so incessantly; she stops trying to wipe them away. William George, now eleven has the responsibility of being the eldest boy. He is standing with his hands straight by his side, not crying, not looking at anyone. His eyes stare into the distance as if his body is at his father's graveside but his mind is elsewhere. Nine-year-old Lilian is holding Lizzie's hand, she covers her eyes with the other. Six-year-old Margaret, named after my mother, is holding my hand and crying softly. She hasn't stopped crying since David died. Five-year-old David is standing with his Uncle John, fidgeting and pulling at his clothes. Looking at him, I wonder if he quite understands what has happened. David made a Will in 1868. He has a life assurance policy with a company in

Melbourne. When Ernest is stronger, I am taking the children back to Melbourne.

"I David Francis McBeth, (sic) being in good bodily health and in possession of my mental faculties do hereby make this my last Will and Testament. Wherein I do will and bequest to my beloved wife Elizabeth McBeth all my real and personal property and effects of whatever kind together with the sum of five hundred pounds £500 effected on my life, and payable after my decease, at the office of the Alliance Insurance Company of Melbourne, in the Colony of Victoria." [1]

Author's note: It is unclear when the "a" was added to the surname, McBeth, and by whom.

Nelson, New Zealand, June 1876

Winter in Nelson is more ferocious than winter in Melbourne. June is the wettest month of the year. It was raining when I got out of bed to see to my youngest child. His habit was to grizzle around 6am for my attention. The other children had been out of the crib by his age, but he was small and while he occupied the crib, he would sleep in my room. This morning he didn't cry, and I slept until seven. With a rush of fear I jumped out of bed and went to his side. From the colour of his skin I don't think he had been dead for long. I put my hand on his cheek; it was as cold as the stone on David's grave. I wrapped a blanket around my shoulders and went to the kitchen looking for my mother-in-law.

'It's a miserable day,' she said when she saw me. I stood in the doorway, unable to move, unable to cry, unable to speak.

'Elizabeth what is it?'

I nodded toward my bedroom.

Susan pushed passed me. Her wailing when she found Ernest, woke the rest of the house.

It was still raining.

It rained two days later when we buried the tiny little boy with his father.

I wanted to believe David, to have hope our little boy would improve. It's as if the infant lost the will to live after his father died. It's as if David took the child's essence with him in January. Ernest is resting with his father. They will keep each other company until I join them.

I am packing up our belongings, selling the house, and John is buying David's share of the business. My children and I will return to Melbourne. Apart from the grave of my husband and infant son, there is nothing to keep us in New Zealand. My wonderful husband ran his business efficiently and has left enough funds for me to buy a house in Melbourne and educate our children. I won't have to take in mending or dressmaking to feed and clothe them. My children and I won't be destitute like my mother was when our Papa lost the farm at Greenhills and took us to Collingwood to live. Mine and David's children won't be living in Collingwood. Thanks to his foresight and good management, our children will live in a nice home in a good neighbourhood.

34

CAROLINE BULMER (NEE BLAY)

Life on a mission station in Gippsland.
"John Bulmer (1833-1913), missionary and clergyman, came to
Australia in 1852 and worked as a cabinetmaker in Melbourne for two
years before going to the goldfields. Here he witnessed the 'wicked
way in which the Aborigines were treated' and decided to help them
by volunteering for missionary work. In 1855, he was sent to assist in
establishing a mission station at Yelta, west of Mildura on the Murray
River. Here, he married schoolteacher Marianne Stocks. He remained
at Yelta until returning to Melbourne where Marianne died in early
1861. Bulmer then travelled to Gippsland and, guided by local
Aboriginal men, selected a site for a mission station at Lake Tyers.
Bulmer is believed to have chosen the site for its isolation from white
settlement; its distance from 'auriferous areas'; and because it would
enable the station a degree of self-sufficiency as a favoured hunting
and fishing place for the local Kurnai people. Bulmer and his second
wife, Caroline (née Blay, d. 1918) commenced work at the Lake Tyers
Mission Station in 1862, building a church, school, and houses for the
residents while also encouraging them to maintain some traditional
customs and practices. Bulmer operated somewhat independently of
the Victorian Board for the Protection of Aborigines and was

sometimes engaged in disagreements with them - notably over the introduction of the Aborigines Protection Act (1886), which threatened to split a number of Lake Tyers families. Bulmer was ordained as an Anglican priest in 1904. In 1907, the Board removed him from the position of manager of the Lake Tyers station, reluctantly permitting him to remain there for 'religious duties' until his death in 1913. Despite his typical evangelical zeal, Bulmer was unusual among his missionary contemporaries for recognising the merits of Aboriginal customs and laws. A sympathetic and accurate observer of Aboriginal life, Bulmer's personal papers are now in the collection of Museum Victoria and are considered among the most important early accounts of Kurnai culture."
https://www.portrait.gov.au/people/john-bulmer-1833

Lake Tyers, Gippsland 1877

My dear sister, Elizabeth,

Mama has told me of your very sad news. My heart breaks for you my dear, but take comfort in the Lord, and believe you will see your beloved husband and infant son again.
John and I keep you in our prayers.

I am happy you have returned to Victoria and although it is a long way from Melbourne to Lake Tyers, but not as far as New Zealand, I hope we can see each other soon. I would like you to meet mine and John's children. And we would love to see yours.

You know of our first three children, the boys, William, now fourteen, John, eleven, and Robert nine. Since you were in New Zealand we have been blessed with another son, Richard Douglas, who is eight, and our first daughter, Frances Amy, who is now five. I chose the same name as our delightful sister, Frances Amy, believing a kindred spirit would be shared. Henry, born in 1873 is now four. I am again with child, the infant expected early next year. It is a busy life. However, I am very fortunate to have the help of my Aboriginal sisters. They help look after the children and support me when I give birth (which is Heaven sent when the midwife isn't available).

John is kept occupied with his work with the Aborigines and is often in conflict with the Victorian Board for the Protection of Aborigines. It upsets him to see the people treated badly, and he does what he can to keep them living the life they know.

Mama tells me you are buying a house in Hawthorn. Please send me your address so we can keep corresponding.

I pray you will stay well and strong, and that we will see each other again, soon.

Your loving sister,
Caroline

35

ELIZABETH

Milestones for Melbourne

"Melbourne celebrates the growth of its trade and industry with an Intercolonial Exhibition.
In 1873, riots occur in Clunes in Victoria due to the use of Chinese miners to break a miners' strike; the violence forced the Chinese people to return to Ballarat.
Most government-assisted immigration ceases, following an economic downturn.
The Colonial Land and Emigration Commission in England closes, and the colonies take over the selection and administration of immigrants.
The Australian Natives Association is formed to represent the interests of the expanding Australian-born population.
In 1875, the last convict hulk anchored off Port Phillip Bay is retired and sold off.
A further four Aboriginal missions are established around Victoria."
https://museumsvictoria.com.au/longform/immigration-to-victoria/#1870s
"Government House
Completed in 1876, Victoria's Government House is one of the largest

and most beautiful mansion houses in Australia and one of the finest examples of nineteenth-century residential architecture.
Royal Arcade
Opened in 1870, this was Melbourne's first shopping arcade, and is the oldest still standing in Australia. It was designed in the Italian Renaissance Revival style by Charles Webb"
https://whatsonblog.melbourne.vic.gov.au/historic-buildings-to-explore/

Burwood Road, Hawthorn 1878.

It's been twelve years since David and I and Lizzie and William left Melbourne. The children don't remember it. Their home, until recently was New Zealand. They all have the accent that identifies them as not quite from Melbourne. When they speak I notice people listen to pick up where they are from.

The changes to this city are extraordinary. When I was a child, Melbourne was dirt streets and timber, ramshackle buildings with the odd stone one here and there. Now there are handsome buildings in the city centre. A General Post Office building on the corner of Elizabeth and Bourke Streets has become a meeting point, an exhibition building is being constructed in the Carlton Gardens to host the Melbourne International Exhibition in 1880. Parliament House in Spring Street is still in construction even though it had started when we were living in Collingwood. And a quaint shopping arcade 'The Royal Arcade' has opened in Collins Street. I will take Mama there for her birthday.

David's mother, Susan, writes every few months. She misses the children. I told her when we left New Zealand last year she was welcome to come to Melbourne and live with us. I think she feels obligated to David's brothers John and William. It was difficult to leave her, but I couldn't bear the thought of living in Nelson without my beloved David. Not a day goes by that I don't see him smiling at me with those blue twinkling eyes, or picking up and hugging the younger children, tickling them until they beg him to stop.

Mama's friendship with Joseph McGinty didn't survive. He sold the house they lived in, along with all his other properties and went back to Ireland. He wanted Mama to go with him, but she declined. My sister Maggie is still unmarried and has bought the house she was renting, at 76 Moray Place, South Melbourne. She is teaching. Mama has moved in with her. They will be good for each other. Even if Maggie marries, Mama will still have somewhere to live. It breaks my heart to see her relying on her children for a roof over her head. Papa left her with nothing. Mama used to tell us stories about how grand-mama Catherine took Mama and her sister, Sadie from one place to the other. Sometimes they stayed with our great grandmama, Eliza-beth, other times with our grandmama and grandpapa Sarah and James. Great grandmama Elizabeth spent the last few years of her life moving between her daughters' homes because our great grandpapa, James, died leaving many debts. She had to sell the house he built her. When I remember these stories it makes me thankful David came into my life. I won't ever have to worry about where I will live. I bought this house with the life assurance David left me.

'Mama,' Lizzie interrupted my daydreaming when she pushed open the parlour door. 'You are napping again. Ethel won't get ready for bed. She's complaining it's too early. I really can't be bothered with her.'

My eldest daughter stood in the doorway between the parlour and the hall, with her arms folded across her chest and a scowl on her face that would make the dog run and hide.

'There's no need to be so dramatic about these small events, Lizzie. I will tend to Ethel.'

Walking into the bedroom Ethel shared with Margaret, I saw evidence of the child's confrontation with her older sister. The four-year-old had crumpled her nightclothes on the floor, spilled the water from the washbasin onto the sideboard, and thrown herself on the bed. She was curled up in a little ball, her arms around her legs bringing her knees up under her chin. Her golden curls were tumbling over the pillow as if just released from weeks tied up in a bun. The movement of her body with the sobs that follow sustained crying had me wiping tears from my eyes.

'What is wrong, Ethel? Why are you so upset?' I asked her.

Between sobs, she stammered, 'I asked Lizzie if she missed Papa and she screamed at me that I wouldn't even remember Papa, so why would I ask her that. She was sad, so I thought she was thinking of Papa. She didn't have to scream at me.'

Sitting next to her on the bed, she released her curled up legs, and climbed onto my lap, still sobbing. 'It's alright, Ethel. I'll speak to Lizzie. She shouldn't have screamed at you. But you must remember that the older children do think of Papa and they do miss him. Now, let's get you ready for bed.'

Lizzie and William knew their father well and missed his generous and loving nature. They both took some time to adjust to his death. I delayed leaving New Zealand until I thought they were ready to leave the town they'd grown up in, and to leave their father behind in the cemetery. I don't think Lizzie will ever recover from the death of her father, followed six months later by the death of baby Ernest.

William seems to be trying to fill the void his father left behind. At the end of school each day he sits Lilian, Margaret and David at the table in the kitchen and has them go over the lessons they did at school, telling him what they learned. His own father did this with Lizzie and he when they started school in Nelson. William organises the children's chores and makes sure their rooms are tidy. Collecting eggs and looking after the hens he has delegated to seven-year-old David, and Ethel. Lilian and Margaret pick and wash vegetables from the garden and set the table for supper each evening. He and Lizzie clear the table and help with the dishes.

The children David and I brought into this world are a blessing. I'm sure he would be proud of them.

1880

My eldest son, William has taken on the responsibilities of a father figure in our household. At fifteen he is taller than me and has his father's ability to organise and manage. Margaret, nine-years, is in awe of her older brother and seeks his approval for school work, needlework, cooking, and always seeks his permission when she is leaving the house. I am fortunate that William is such a strong and willing support.

The Melbourne International Exhibition is to be held at the new Exhibition Building in the Carlton Gardens in the next few weeks, and William has asked permission to attend. How can I deny him after all the work he does for the family? I'll travel by train into Melbourne next week and withdraw some money from the bank for William to spend at the Exhibition.

1881

My dear older sister, Maggie has at forty-five found a man to marry. She hasn't told us anything about him, just that they are good for each other, and make each other happy. I am thrilled to see her so jubilant. It means she will have to stop teaching, though. Married women in Victoria can't work in schools.

My son, William, will escort Maggie on her wedding day. Each month that passes my oldest son grows even more into a capable, caring, man, just like his father.

My youngest sister, Frances Amy has told me frequently she has no intention of marrying. She has opened a private school at 118 Tope Street, South Melbourne, and is doing very well. [1]

Mama is intrigued by the success and happiness of her daughters, and dismayed at the behaviour of her son, William James Blay. William's wife left him not long after the birth of their third child, Amy Caroline McMurray Blay. He hasn't seen his wife, daughter or surviving son, James Douglas, since. Mama says he reminds her of her step-father, James Blay Jr, and wonders if Papa's affliction has been passed to William James. We have not heard from him since he attacked his mother-in-law ten years ago.

"A brutal son-in-law. A respectable old lady complained that her son-in-law, one William James Blay, had used threatening language towards her, and that she was in fear of bodily injury. The defendant would not work, and his conduct was such that his wife refused to live with him. He amused himself with going to his mother-in-law's house and breaking clocks, and putting blankets and sheets upon the fire. Blay promised that it should not occur again, and stated he was going into the country. He was ordered to find one surety of £10 that he would keep the peace for six months." [2]

My younger brother, John Douglas followed Caroline to Lake Tyers, and is still unmarried. He helps my brother-in-law John Bulmer in the mission work with the Aborigines. Even as an adult he doesn't look healthy. He was a sickly baby and child, and Mama fretted over him. He survived childhood. Mama did well looking after him.

36

MARGARET

1880s Melbourne

"Visitors to Melbourne in the 1880s were amazed. Here in the
Southern Hemisphere was a city larger than most European capitals.
In just a decade the population had doubled, racing to half-a-million.
Citizens strutted the streets, bursting with pride as their city boomed.
While Sydney was seen as slow and steady, Melbourne was fast and
reckless. Ornate office buildings up to 12 storeys high rivalled those of
New York, London and Chicago. Money was poured into lavishly
decorated banks, hotels and coffee palaces. Towers, spires, domes and
turrets reached to the skies."
https://museumsvictoria.com.au/marvellous/1880s/

Saturday 12 January 1884

The New Year began with a huge celebration outside the GPO in
Elizabeth Street in Melbourne. Margaret didn't attend, her
eyesight was failing. She thought it was because of all the years she'd
spent sitting in poor light mending clothes and dressmaking, and she

found it difficult to get on and off the train. Her grandson, William, now nineteen and a very tall, strong-looking young man, sat opposite her in the parlour of her daughter Maggie's house telling her all about the New Year festivities. She hadn't been into the city for about four years, the last time was when Elizabeth took her shopping at the Royal Arcade for her birthday. She was interested to hear how things were changing.

'It's a very busy place, Grandmama,' he told her. 'I will open a business there when I'm older. I'm going to be a successful businessman like my father. When I go back to New Zealand I'll ask my Uncles John and William about expanding my business there. Did you know the city of Melbourne is bigger than some European capitals, Grandmama? I'm going to Europe one day, too.'

While William stopped to take a breath, Margaret smiled. She knew her grandson would do what he said, he had plans laid out for his life and being wealthy and successful was a priority. She saw his father, David Francis in this young man. He held himself as his father did, tall and proud, he had the same Irish/Scottish colouring of his father and the same twinkle in his eye. Elizabeth marrying David was a blessing. Although their marriage had been short, Elizabeth was happy in it, and their union had produced six surviving, exceptional children.

There was no-one to ask as Margaret wondered about the flaws in the sons of James and Sarah Blay. Their eldest, her step-father James Jr, spent time in prison, and treated her mother badly until he ultimately deserted her and his six-month-old infant. William was declared insolvent in New Norfolk and he lost Stoney Bank Farm. They absconded to Port Phillip forty-one years ago, only to then lose Greenhills Station on the River Plenty because William had over extended and the bank repossessed the farm. William then became lost to the world and died in the insane asylum. Her brother-in-law, John appears to have deserted his wife, Elizabeth and the family, the youngest child just eight-years-old when he left. She shook her head in dismay.

'What is it, Grandmama?' her grandson asked.

'Nothing, dear. I was wondering about the things that affect people in their lives. Why don't you see about making me a cup of tea?' Watching William leave the room, Margaret smiled the inner smile of comfort, this boy seems to be more a McBeath than a Blay.

'We are sitting out on the back verandah Grandmama,' William said coming back into the parlour, 'Come along, I'll help you. Mama and Aunt Frances are making the tea.'

Margaret let her grown up responsible grandson help her out of the chair and marvelled at his manners when he put her arm through his, leading her to the back verandah.

Fourteen-year-old Margaret Frances helped her brother settle their grandmama into a rocking chair in the shade. The bond between this brother and sister is strong, Margaret thought. I hope they live close to each other when they have families of their own, like Sadie and I did in New Norfolk.

Her daughters Frances Amy and Elizabeth brought afternoon tea onto the verandah. The heat of the day dissipated when the wind changed, bringing with it a cool breeze that pushed the suffocating high temperature out of the suburb towards the north. Margaret liked living near the Bay, the sea breeze in summer made the oppressing Melbourne heat more bearable.

This Saturday afternoon Elizabeth had brought the children for a visit, and Frances had her cook prepare biscuits and cakes. Margaret relished having Elizabeth's children nearby. Caroline's nine surviving children she had never seen. Caroline kept her informed of their milestones through letters, but they would never know the love of a grandmother's embrace. The same could be said for Sarah Susanna's nine children, all growing up in Sydney, never to see their cousins or their Grandmama or Aunts.

Elizabeth's eldest, Lizzie was twenty-one, and like Frances Amy seemed to have no interest in finding a husband. William had taken charge of the family and would do everything he said he would. Sixteen-year-old Lilian was a stunning, tall, dark-haired girl who reminded Margaret of her mother, Catherine. Fourteen-year-old Margaret Frances followed her older brother around like a lost puppy. David, thirteen, and Ethel, ten, rounded out Elizabeth's brood. Margaret closed her eyes and put her head on the back of the chair. Relaxing while the chair rocked quietly, she listened to the chatter of the surrounding family, feeling blessed she was here with them.

Saturday 19 January 1884

Elizabeth took the two youngest children, David Francis and Ethel, to visit Margaret.

Frances Amy met her sister on the front verandah and told the children she would take them to see the hatched ducklings. 'Maggie wants to speak to you, Elizabeth,' she said as she walked toward the pond with a child holding onto each hand.

Walking into the house, Elizabeth felt dread creep up her back. It was a warm summer's day, but she shivered. 'Maggie,' she called into the hallway.

Her sister was an ample, forty-eight-year-old woman. She held tight onto the railing on the stairs as she made her way down. Her hair was piled loosely on her head in the latest fashion, and her dress came in at the waist with buttons from the waistband to the neckline. The buttons around her bosom looked as if they were about to pop.

Elizabeth watched her sister's expression change as she neared the foot of the stairs. Maggie's brief show of delight at seeing her sister, changed to a solemn concern the closer she came to the end of the stairs.

'Mama is unwell. The doctor has been, and he says she has a chest infection and that she has had it for some time. He left medicine to aid her breathing, but it doesn't seem to help. You go up to her, and I'll make her some lemon tea.'

Elizabeth gasped when she walked into her mother's bedroom. Margaret lay in the bed, the covers pulled up to her chin, and her skin almost as white as the pillow her head rested on.

Margaret opened her eyes when Elizabeth moved a chair to the side of the bed. 'Ah, you are here. Tell Maggie I won't want the tea and that I love her. Tell Frances Amy I'm proud of her, and when you write to Sarah Susanna, Caroline, John Douglas and William James, tell them I love them. Give each of your wonderful children a kiss for me and know I love you too. I will sleep now.'

Margaret Tedder's eyes closed as she remembered a life of happiness, sadness, change, upheaval, misery and accomplishment.

37

ELIZABETH

January 1885

My health hasn't been good the last few months, and this summer has taken what little energy I have, thrown it onto the street and kicked it away. I haven't felt this unwell since I was carrying Ernest Douglas. My older daughters have noticed that I'm not up to my usual chores and activities, but the boys are oblivious. Lizzie has been bringing me cups of tea in bed in the morning before I get up and making sure Margaret, Ethel, and David attend school. Margaret will finish school this year.

William is running the finances of the household; still filling the father figure void left by David. Losing Mama last January was hard on William, he had become close to her since our return from New Zealand. He gets the train to St Kilda and takes flowers to her grave at the St Kilda cemetery every couple of weeks. Such a caring young man, so like his father. I miss David.

I have said nothing to my children, but my sisters, Frances and Maggie know of the severity of my illness. The doctor says I have cancer of the breast[1] and he doesn't expect me to live much longer. Maggie and Frances will support my children. Margaret and Ethel attend Frances' school in South Melbourne, she will help look after them. Lizzie and Lilian are grown women and will look after David and the girls when they are home from school. William will keep it all together.

I could feel sorry for myself, sorry for my children. But I won't. Compared with my mother I have had an amazing life. I married the man of my dreams who treated me like a queen who provided for me and our children so well, that even after his death I had no concerns over money or welfare. Two big men dressed in white uniforms took my father away when I was seven. I watched them carry him out the door. I watched Mama close the door behind him. She didn't even wait to see if he turned to say goodbye. We never saw him again. There isn't even a grave to visit him and lay flowers like William does for my Mama. My heart aches when I think of my Papa and how he left his family and this life. Over the years I had asked Mama to tell me the story of what happened to Papa; her answer was always the same, 'He lost all his money, two properties, and his mind.' She would never add to that summary of her husband's life.

William will make sure I have a headstone and a grave for him and his siblings to visit and lay flowers. I am saddened that I will never see any grandchildren. My time for this world will soon be finished.

Saturday, 7 February 1885

I haven't been able to get out of bed for the last ten days. My strength has evaporated with the summer heat. Lizzie has been trying to force me to drink lemon cordial and to eat some soup. She is a stalwart and isn't giving up easily. The sickness is eating me alive. I can feel it spreading through my body, and as the days progress, it takes more of me with it. My mind is still intact. I've asked Lizzie to call everyone to my bedside. I want to tell them for the last time how much I love each of them, how proud I am of them all, and how their father would be amazed at what wonderful people they had become.

As I look into their faces, watching the signs of grief weigh on them, I see David, holding our infant son, Ernest Douglas. He moves from the window and stands beside the bed. Reaching out to touch his hand and the face of my baby boy, David grasps my arm and helps me out of the bed. Holding my hand he leads me away with him. Looking back at my children I see they are all crying. Ethel has thrown herself on my body begging me not to go. David Jr sits on a chair, his hands covering the tears streaming down his face. William has the same posture and look on his face he did the day of his father's funeral. Margaret is standing as close as possible to William, unmoving, no expression. Lizzie and Lilian are hugging each other.

I will miss them, they will miss me. But it is my time to go.

2

"McBeath – On the 7th February, at her residence, Albert Park, after a long and painful illness, Elizabeth, widow of the late D.F. McBeath, late of New Zealand, and fourth daughter of the late Margaret Blay of South Melbourne, aged 42 years."[3]

38

MARGARET FRANCES MCBEATH

Maturity
"Although the tough, weathered, hard-drinking bushmen of the kind
mythologised by writers like Banjo Paterson and Henry Lawson are
popularly associated with the character of late nineteenth century
Australia, it was also a time when alternative ideas about identity
began to come into play. Like earlier ideals of masculinity, these ideas
are traceable through the changes in facial hair fashions adopted by
Australian men. The period between the 1850s and the 1880s may
have been the era of beards as badges of the wise, protective,
resourceful or vigorous. But the decades that followed might be
considered those when dignified restraint and greater attention to
grooming took precedence and when, in Australia, the rugged, anti-
authoritarian bushman began to be replaced by the urbane,
responsible and educated chap.
An increasing emphasis on tidiness and tailoring was characteristic
of men's fashions in Britain and America in this era. Beards retained
some popularity, but were more commonly seen in trimmer, more
manicured or sober styles."
https://www.portrait.gov.au

May 1885

N ot only am I heart-broken at the death of my beloved mother, but William has gone to London to look for partners in a business venture. He promised me he would come home. He only planned to be away for three to four years. Mama said William would look after us, look after the finances, the house, our lives, but he said he has a life of his own to build. He said building a fortune would help us all in the future. I don't see how. I miss him. I miss Mama.

This is my last year of school. My sister, Ethel and I are very fortunate to attend the private school our aunt, Mama's sister, Frances Amy Blay started in South Melbourne. We board there during the week. Aunt Frances has rooms for us on the second floor where she has her private rooms. At the weekend we go home to our family in Albert Park where our eldest sister Lizzie, and our second eldest sister, Lilian, live and care for David Jr who is fourteen and at day school. Mama sold the Hawthorn house three years before she died and bought the house in Albert Park. The suburb is next to South Melbourne where my aunts live.

Lizzie is a talented artist. She paints pictures of the Melbourne suburbs and sells them so that she has her own income. She says when David Jr has left home, she will teach like our Aunt Frances. Lilian is a milliner,[1] she makes the most exquisite hats for the ladies from the wealthy neighbourhood. I don't know what I will do when I finish school. Mama said I was a talented dressmaker, but I remember watching Grandmama sitting in the window's light sewing tiny buttons on to garments made of fabric that slid around in her hands. I don't have the patience.

1888

I got out of bed early this morning to get the tram to Port Melbourne to greet William. He arrives today from his time in England. There is much to tell him. Our brother, David Francis, seventeen has moved to Bendigo. He is working in a gold mine. He made plans to leave Melbourne when we received William's letter to say he was on his way home. David knows William would object to this line of employment and life-style and would try to stop him. Lilian is in her own shop, working as a milliner. She lives in a flat above the shop in St Kilda. Ethel is still at school.

The clouds hang like a shroud over the rising sun, teasing with intermittent breaks to reveal a day that could be glorious if the clouds blow away and allow it to be so. I have grown to be fond of autumn in Melbourne. The trees brought in from England have leaves that change colour and drop on the roads and footpaths creating carpets of gold, orange and yellow. Even at my age it is entertaining to kick the leaves as one walks along the path. Waiting at the tram stop with Lizzie and Ethel I take my excitement at seeing William out on the piles of leaves at the foot of the trees, by kicking them onto the road. Lizzie chastises me for being too old for such behaviour.

William strides off the ship as if he is one of the owners. He is dressed like a man in a fashion advertisement in one newspaper. He is clean shaven except for a moustache, his hair is short, he is wearing a white shirt with a collar that stands up on its own, a black bow tie, a grey woollen suit and a long, black woollen overcoat. My first thought is that the overcoat won't be on his back for long, the clouds are releasing their hold on the sun's rays. When he sees us, he waves. We wave back. I'm sure my wave is more vigorous than Lizzie's or Ethel's. There is a man walking next to him, talking to him. This man sees someone on the wharf waiting, and waves too.

William drops his bag on the wharf and holds out his arms as I run to him. I feel like a six-year-old child running to meet her father. His grin is the last thing I see as I bury my face in his embrace and cry.

'Why are you crying, Margaret,' he asks, 'I am home, no need to be sad.'

I notice a roundness to his intonation. Pushing myself away from his embrace I comment on his accent. 'You sound like one of the

British people who pretend they own all of Melbourne,' I scold. 'You didn't sound like that when you left.'

Smiling at me, William kisses my cheek and reaches out to hug Lizzie and Ethel. The man who accompanied William off the ship is standing to the side with his arm around a woman. The man coughs to get William's attention.

'Aah,' says William. 'Ladies,' he calls my sisters and me, 'this is a friend of mine David Mackie, and his lovely wife Minnie Jane. I'm having a welcome home party Friday week, and David and Minnie Jane will be on the guest list.'

We three greet William's friends politely and he then bids them farewell. Swamping our brother with questions as we drag him toward the tram, he stops and says indignantly 'I'm not getting a tram all the way to Hawthorn. I'll hail a carriage.'

Lizzie wouldn't let us take a carriage to the Port, she said we needed to be careful not to waste our money. I don't think that matters now William is back.

Our home in Albert Park hadn't experienced this much happiness since before Mama died. William invited friends we didn't know he had, to his welcome home party. David Mackie arrived with Minnie Jane, his wife, and she brought someone else too. I am introduced to him, Charles Mark Werrett, her younger brother. We are all introduced to someone else that I immediately feel a pang of jealousy towards, Annie McHutchison. William announces that he and Annie are getting married.

Charles is two years younger than me, but his presence exudes a confidence that belies his sixteen years. He invited me to take a walk with him in the Botanic Gardens next Saturday afternoon. He is a bootmaker and finishes work at noon. I am looking forward to it.

1889

Charles accompanied me to William's wedding. William married Annie on 10th June. It was a dignified event, with close family and friends, held in Annie's parents' home in Balwyn. Her parents came from Scotland in 1853 for the Gold Rush and still have a Scottish accent that is very hard to understand. Charles said he heard Annie's father talking to another guest about the fortune he made on the goldfields. I looked carefully at Annie's dress. I think she is already with child.

December 1889

My brother William arrived at our home in Albert Park with the agony of grief carved into his brow. His eyes were so puffy he looked like the frogs our brother David used to catch by the river. Thousands of tears left stains on his cheeks. He sat at the kitchen table and hid his face in his hands while Ethel and I waited, not knowing whether to interrupt his sorrow.

'What has happened, William?' I found the courage to ask.

Through sobs that would not abate, William said Annie had given birth to a baby girl who they named Florence Jeannie. 'She lived for one hour,' he whispered 'one hour and then she was gone. She was beautiful. Dark hair like Annie's, blue eyes like our Papa's and I swear she had Mama's nose.' Ethel and I each put an arm around William's shoulders and stayed with him until the tears dried up.

31st January 1890

Charles and I are marrying today at the Wesleyan Church in Balwyn.[2] He is eighteen, and I'm twenty. Already with an established boot making business in Balwyn, he is mature beyond his years and more than capable of looking after me and any future children. He has grown a moustache which tickles when he kisses me. He said his Papa had a moustache and he wanted to emulate his success in business and his status as a gentleman. It was clear to me that Charles had adored his father, but until a week before our wedding, he hadn't spoken of his family.

We sat on the bench seat on the front porch swatting away mosquitoes and sipping lemon cordial the night before our wedding, when Charles shared his family story. 'We are getting married,' he said. 'You should know the events of my life that have made me the man I am today.'

I had been very selective about the parts of my family story I'd shared with him, and that sent a shiver of guilt running up my spine. I had told him my mother's family came from Tasmania, but not that her parents both had convict fathers, or that my great grandparents three times were also transported convicts. Mama had said that was an old story and we were no longer associated with that tardy connection to our past. I don't think Charles would have been concerned, but William didn't want us to talk about our Tasmanian family and we did as he asked.

39

RICHARD WERRETT

"Rangeworthy is a semi-rural farming village in South Gloucestershire, England, nearby communities include Falfield and Charfield. The village population taken at the 2011 census was 675. The village lies between Iron Acton and Bagstone, along the B4058 road."

https://en.wikipedia.org/wiki/Rangeworthy

"The surge of wealth and people cemented Melbourne's future as a major city. By 1861, just 25 years after John Batman set up the township, it was home to 125,000 people. Gold sparked the development of housing, schools, churches, fine homes for professional people and merchants, and public buildings. "

https://www.onlymelbourne.com.au/history-of-melbourne-581#.W9KqgeKYPbo

"The latter half of the 19th century proved an economically prosperous and exciting time for Melbourne and Victoria. With the

Victorian Gold Rush beginning in 1851 and running into the late 1860s, Victoria dominated the world's gold output, and in one decade the population rose from 75,000 to over 500,000, with some places seeing a 3000% increase. Victoria suffered from an acute labour shortage despite its steady influx of migrants, and this pushed up wages until they were the highest in the world. During these years, Victoria was known as the 'working man's paradise', and people from all around the world migrated to Melbourne hoping to find their riches in the Gold Rush."

http://www.eng.unimelb.edu.au/about/history/1860s
"The Burke and Wills expedition was an expedition organised by the Royal Society of Victoria in Australia in 1860–61 of 19 men, led by Robert O'Hara Burke and William John Wills, with the objective of crossing Australia from Melbourne in the south, to the Gulf of Carpentaria in the north, a distance of around 3,250 kilometres (approximately 2,000 miles). At that time most of the inland of Australia had not been explored by non-Indigenous people and was largely unknown to the European settlers. The expedition left Royal Park, Melbourne on 20th August 1860."

https://en.wikipedia.org/wiki/Burke_and_Wills_expedition

When Richard Werrett was born in Rangeworthy, Gloucestershire in 1832, his parents, Mark, and Ann (Window) were living in the same district they'd both been born in. He was the last of ten children and learned quickly about being self-sufficient as older siblings died before their time. His brother, Mark, born in 1829, died in 1837 at eight. Richard was five. His sister, Caroline, born in 1821, died in 1843 at twenty-two. Richard was eleven. When Caroline died, Richard made a promise to himself that he would not die in the same place he was born in. He wanted to see what the world offered.

On the 25th June 1858, nine months after his marriage to Mary Jane Williams, on 17 September 1857, Richard took Mary's hand and helped her off the *Monsoon*[1] on to the jetty in Melbourne, Victoria, Australia. The start of their new life away from Gloucestershire and the staid situation of his parents and siblings, began this day.

1860

Richard held Mary Ann's hand as she fed their baby daughter, Minnie Jane, for the first time. The child, the first of the new generation born in the Colony of Victoria, had dark hair, brown eyes and fair skin. 'She will be healthy, born in the new world,' Richard told his wife. 'You must write to our parents and tell them about their granddaughter.'

A wave of sadness washed over Mary's face when Richard mentioned their parents. 'Our parents will see no grandchildren born on this side of the world,' she said to Richard.

'They have many more from our brothers and sisters,' he smiled. 'Today we begin a new family dynasty.'

'Bundle the little one up against the cold, Mary, we are going to Royal Park to see Robert O'Hara Burke leave on his expedition to explore Australia, at 12 o'clock today.'[2]

"Three cheers having been given for the party, and for Mr. Burke, the meeting separated.

The following are the names of the members of the expedition, vis :- Richard O'Hara Burke, leader ; George James Landells, in charge of the camels, and second in command ; William James Wills, third in command ; Thomas Beckler, medical officer; Ludwig Becker, artist, naturalist, geological direct, etc.; Charles Ferguson, foreman; and Thomas McDonough,

William, Pattons, Patrick Langan, Owen Cowen, William Brahs, Robert
Fletcher, John King, Henry Croker and John Drakesford, associates.
The expedition will start from the Royal Park about 12 o'clock this day."

Mary Ann put a bonnet on her baby she'd knitted while expecting. She wrapped her up tight in a blanket her mother had packed for her as a reminder of England. Richard draped Mary Ann's coat over her shoulders, slid his arms into his, and walked with her outside to hail a horse and buggy.

'Minnie won't remember this day, Mary Ann, but we will. This is the day the expedition to explore the centre of Australia left Melbourne. We are here to witness it. This is history. We are making history.' His face shone with the glory of the expedition and the excitement of bearing witness. Not as enamoured with the significance of the day, Mary Ann took her husband's hand and followed him to the expedition point.

1862

When Richard and Mary Ann arrived in Melbourne, Richard had a tidy sum of money saved. In England he had worked at whatever would give him a wage enough to pay his father board, and to save to travel to Victoria. Since arriving in the new Colony he had established a gardening business, had many customers and his dream of owning a house in Melbourne was but one or two years away.

The birth of Richard and Mary Ann's first son in 1862, happened in their rented home in Balwyn. Frederick William had fair hair and blue eyes, with a dark tinge to his skin. 'He is the opposite of Minnie in his colouring,' Richard said to Mary Ann. 'He is like your side of the family.' After the infant had suckled his fill for the first time, Richard took his son from his wife and sat in the rocking chair by the fire. His face glowed with both happiness and the warmth from the flames.

'What is that?' Minnie, now two, demanded of her father when the midwife brought her into her parents' bedroom.

'This is your baby brother, Minnie. Mama has given me a son and you a brother. Are you not happy?'

Minnie shrugged her shoulders and climbed up onto the bed to snuggle with her mother. 'Mama is mine,' she said.

4 June 1864

Minnie, not old enough to look after her two-year-old brother while her mother was in labour, ran to the neighbour's for help. 'Mama is crying. She said the baby is coming,' Minnie told her neighbour when the door opened. 'It's early. Mama isn't ready.'

The neighbour's husband, a salesman, hadn't yet left for work. He went to fetch the midwife while his wife rushed to Mary Ann's side.

Florence Louisa, the third Werrett child born in the Colony was healthy, loud and pink.

'Why is she pink?' Minnie demanded of the midwife.

'She is supposed to be pink. Go to the kitchen and get things ready to make your Mama a cup of tea. I have more to do. That one is full of confidence,' the midwife muttered as she helped Mary Ann.

'Papa, Papa, Mama has given you another girl. A girl like me.' Minnie gushed when her father walked in the door.

'We are building a new dynasty,' Richard smiled at Mary Ann as she rested in their bed, the baby girl by her side. 'And I have more exciting news for the day,' he said 'I have bought a house close to here, in Balwyn Road. We now have our own home in our new country, with our new babies.'

Richard's gardening business flourished with the growth of homes in Melbourne. The well-to-do had modern, brick and bluestone cottages built, and then used the services of enterprising men like Richard to complete their gardens.

Whilst some had rushed off to the goldfields on arrival in Melbourne, Richard kept to the plan he had for growing wealth.

. . .

In 1866, Elizabeth Ann Werrett made her way into the world, the first child born in the home Richard had bought. As much as he adored his daughters, Richard hoped another son would soon join the family.

40

MARY ANN WERRETT (NEE WILLIAMS)

1867

W ith four children six and under Mary Ann was grateful her husband had been thrifty enough to save his money, so he could buy the lovely, modern house they lived in. There were three bedrooms, an inside kitchen with attached wet room, and a parlour and dining room. Each room had a fireplace, and until the children were old enough to chop wood, she spent an hour each morning after Richard had left, chopping and carrying wood for the kitchen stove.

Minnie Jane had started her education at the local church school and walked there each morning after she'd helped Mary Ann with Frederick and Florence. The child got Florence dressed and eating her oatmeal while Mary tended to baby Elizabeth. Frederick, although not old enough to cook breakfast, served his own and with Minnie's help got dressed for the day. When Mary Ann saw Minnie off to school, the seven-year-old had already completed a morning's work.

Rushing out of bed before the vomit she was trying to hold down gushed from her mouth, Mary Ann ran into the back garden. The sign of another child growing inside her splattered over the brick path Richard had laid to the outhouse. Sitting on the bench Richard had erected and placed to soak up the sun as it swept across the sky from the north, Mary Ann put her head back and tried to take in deep breaths. This would be her fifth child in eight years.

Thursday, 3 September 1868

Ada Alice Werrett made her way into the world with her eight-year-old sister, Minnie Jane acting as midwife. Mary Ann's labour progressed quickly, and the determined infant would not wait for a time to suit her mother.

'Oh, Mama, she is beautiful,' Minnie exclaimed as she watched Mary Ann clean and wrap the infant and cut the cord. Lying back on the bed, Mary Ann explained the next stage of childbirth to her daughter. When the events of the delivery were complete, Mary Ann gave thanks to God that the new baby arrived after her older children had come home from school.

The smile on Richard's face when presented with his fifth daughter made Mary Ann giggle. His face lit up the room like the morning sun creeping through the window curtains. 'Why are you smiling so, Richard?' she asked, 'I thought it would disappoint you having another daughter.'

'How can I be disappointed with a healthy daughter? We will have another son one day. Daughters will look after us in our old age.' He winked at his wife, returned the infant to her arms and told her how beautiful she looked. When Richard left the room to help Minnie and Frederick prepare supper for the children, Mary Ann got out of bed to see what beauty Richard was talking about.

Looking at the woman staring back at her from the mirror, Mary Ann turned around to see if her mother really was in the room, before realising the woman in the mirror was herself. It had been ten years since they'd left Gloucestershire, she wondered if she'd stayed in England would she have aged the same. Had it been the children? Her mother had six children and died at the good age of sixty-five, although Mary Ann remembered the lines around her mother's eyes and the marks of fatigue etched into her cheeks.

Arriving home from work on a winter's evening in 1871, Richard announced to Mary Ann that he was opening a newsvendors in Balwyn Road near the junction of Whitehorse Road. He was tired of working in the mud and cold of winter. The gardening business would be sold.

'Will you be happy working indoors?' she asked. 'After all this baby might be a boy who wants to work in gardens.' Richard brought her close to him and whispered in her ear that this next child would be a boy.

Mary Ann gave birth to Charles Mark Werrett in autumn 1872 while her husband built up his newsvendor's business. Mary Ann's eldest, Minnie Jane now twelve, did everything for the infant except feed him. Once again taking stock of herself in the mirror not long after the birth of a baby, Mary Ann saw an old woman looking at her, a woman who appeared much older than her thirty-five years. She thought the spark that was leaching from her complexion was folding itself into the creases on her face and neck. Thinking each child drained a little more of her life energy, Mary Ann hoped that Richard would be happy with two sons and four daughters. She was tired, whereas Richard was as full of life as ever, and more and more involved in the community. He was so involved in the eight hours movement that his shop was a polling station for ratepayers to vote.

1

Monday 1st July 1878

At forty-one, Mary Ann Werrett gave birth to her fifth son, Graham. The infant took a breath, looked at her with an expression of inevitability as the cord that connected him to his mother was cut, and closed his eyes never to open them again. Mary Ann collapsed back onto the bed, blood gushing from her body, covering any evidence of the little boy making his way into this world. This little boy would wait for her in Heaven with her other two little boys, Herbert John who was born and died in 1874, and Richard Henry who was born and died in 1876.

Barely able to hear the panic in the voices of the people surrounding her, Mary Ann gave into the emptiness that engulfed her almost bloodless body. Her last thought being that Charles was only six.

41

RICHARD WERRETT

1878

Relying on his eldest, Minnie eighteen, to help with the younger children, Charles and Ada, Richard also had the support and help of friends. Alexander Mackie, whose son David had taken a liking to Minnie, and Alexander's wife Jane, who supported Richard with preparation of meals and laundry.

Spending his time growing wealth enabled Richard to immerse himself in thoughts other than those of his loneliness. He missed his wife's smile; her cuddling up to him in bed on a cold winter's night; her putting her cold feet on his backside when she'd been out of bed to one of the children. But above all, he missed her companionship.

Minnie married David Mackie two years after her mother died. It would have overwhelmed Mary Ann with pride. Richard thought she would have struggled to hold back tears of happiness for their daughter.

Mary Ann also missed the birth of their first grandchild, Alexander Mackie, named after David's father, in 1881. She would never see Elsie Jane Mackie born in 1883, or Florence Alice born in 1885. Richard told her when he was lying in bed at night, about the grandchildren, and the stories of their own children. In 1886, Florence married a man called Arthur Ratten. Richard confided in his wife that he didn't like the man, but Florence was adamant he was the one for her.

When Richard died on 3rd April 1888 at the age of fifty-four, he had, by being a good businessman, secured his children's future.

"That the said deceased died possessed of real and personal estate in the Colony of Victoria of the value of three thousand, three hundred and sixty pounds, five shillings. Namely of real estate to the value of three thousand three hundred and sixty-six pounds, and personal estate in the value of eighty-four pounds, five shillings."[1]

In his last will and testament, Richard left his estate divided equally amongst his surviving children.

42

MARGARET FRANCES MCBEATH

Charles worked hard building up his business, and we lived in a small cottage behind his shop in Balwyn Road. He locked the shop over lunch time and came into the cottage to eat with me, always kissing me when he walked in the kitchen, and again when he left. Often he would lead me to our bedroom, carefully remove his jacket, shoes and trousers and wait until I lay on the bed. He would then slide his hands under my dress, pull my underwear down my legs and over my feet, throw them on the floor, and using his fingers, see if I was ready to accept his manhood. When we were first married, neither of us had experienced love-making and we learned together. Now we knew what pleasure was to come from our passion we looked forward to spending time together.

A year after our wedding, I shared the news with Charles that we were to be parents. I knew our frequent love-making would eventually mean babies, but I wasn't sure I was ready to share my husband, although I knew it to be a forgone element of marriage.

Roland Charles was born eleven months after our wedding. William and Annie also had a son, on 5th October 1890: William George after his father. Annie became pregnant again soon after the death of their firstborn. Now little William had a cousin to grow up with.

My brother William and I are the only ones of our brothers and sisters who are married and raising another generation. Lizzie has gone away to the country to teach, David is still in Bendigo, and Lilian and Ethel are living in our family home in Albert Park.

William is now working for Mr Makower's silk trading company in Flinders Lane and establishing a name for himself as an astute businessman. He met Mr Makower on his way home from England. The two men in my life who hold different parts of my heart are proving to be champions of family, business and community.

Our son, Roland has a long face like my Papa had. He has the fair colouring of my Papa and he has my Mama's twinkling blue / grey eyes. He doesn't look like me or Charles. He is a happy little boy who plays with his toys on his own. His favourite activity is to sit in the garden and dig with his toy shovel. Charles bought him a wooden train for his first Christmas, and Roland pushes it around in the dirt in the vegetable garden. When my sister-in-law Annie comes to visit with William George, the two small boys share each other's toys. During one of Annie's afternoon tea visits, I confided in her that I was pregnant with our second child. Getting off her chair quicker than the foxes running away from the hen house when Charles spies them at night, she flung her arms around my shoulders, kissed my cheek, and said 'So am I, Margaret.'

Leslie Francis Werrett, our second son, was born at the end of 1892 a few months before Annie and William's daughter, Constance May. Our families were growing together.

43

CHARLES

Federation

"In 1895 the premiers agreed that another convention should be held, with the delegates directly chosen by the electors. The Federal Convention met in Adelaide in March 1897 and was reconvened in Sydney in September 1897 and Melbourne in January 1898. There were 50 delegates and only Queensland was not represented. A Drafting Committee consisting of Barton, Sir John Downer and Richard O'Connor drafted a Commonwealth of Australia Constitution Bill which, with amendments, was adopted by the Convention. The Bill was then submitted to referenda in New South Wales, Victoria, South Australia and Tasmania. There were majorities in each colony, but only a slim one in New South Wales, where leading politicians such as George Reid remained half-hearted. In January 1899 the premiers made some amendments, mainly at the instigation of New South Wales, and new referenda were held in every colony apart from Western Australia.

In 1900 delegates from the six colonies met Joseph Chamberlain, the Secretary of State for the Colonies, in London. The negotiations resulted in a few slight amendments and the Constitution Bill was then passed by the British Parliament. Queen Victoria gave her assent on 9 July 1900. In the same month a referendum was held in Western Australia and the federationists were victorious. A proclamation was signed by the Queen on 17 September 1900 declaring that on 1 January 1901 the six colonies would be united under the name of Commonwealth of Australia. Lord Hopetoun was appointed Governor General and on 31 December 1900 he commissioned the first Commonwealth Ministry, headed by Edmund Barton. The first Commonwealth Parliament was opened by the Duke of York in Melbourne on 9 May 1901."

https://www.nla.gov.au/selected-library-collections/federation-of-australia

"Celebrations did not focus just on Sydney. From state capitals to country towns, in small communities and tiny rural schools and even on remote outback stations, people joined together to welcome federation. Shops sold souvenirs such as handkerchiefs, teapots, vases, mugs and plates, as well as booklets and badges to commemorate the day. Songs and poems were written in tribute to the new Australian nation.

A big effort was made to involve children in the celebrations because they were seen as the future of the new nation. Children marched in parades and took part in flag-raising ceremonies. They were presented with special certificates and medals to mark federation. At special 'monster' picnics and sports carnivals, children competed in running, skipping, two-legged and sack races.

Federation was truly an Australia-wide festival. The enthusiastic celebrations across the country showed how eagerly Australians welcomed their new nation."

https://getparliament.peo.gov.au/federation/federation-celebrations

1901

The creases around the corners of Charles' mouth deepened as his smile broadened. Watching his family eating breakfast before an exciting day celebrating the Federation of Australia, brought both joy and sadness. The happiness that filled Charles' heart expanded when Roland, eleven, helped Margaret with Pearl

Ethel, six, Phyllis Elizabeth, four, and Doris Margaret, two. Leslie Francis was nine and spent his time outside in the garden; helping his Mama with his annoying little sisters, got in his way of weeding, planting or pruning. Sadness crept into the tiny little gaps left for it in Charles' heart when he remembered what his own parents missed with his siblings, and now with grandchildren.

The talk of a Federation of Australian states was happening when his parents arrived from England in 1858, it would please his father to know it was finally consolidating. Events planned for the City of Melbourne included the parade. After the parade, his family was joining William and Annie and their children at a monster picnic in the Botanic Gardens[1]. Charles wanted his children to remember this important day. Roland, Leslie and Pearl received commemorative certificates from school. Charles would keep them for posterity.

Once the children were organised and the picnic hamper packed with lunch supplies and treats, Margaret and Charles led their family to the tram stop for the trip into the city. The streets filled with people in their best outfits, their smart footwear - Charles always noticed peoples' footwear – big, bright hats and carrying picnic baskets for the celebration of Federation. 'Do you think the children will remember this day?' he asked Margaret. 'Roland, Leslie and Pearl will,' she said, 'the little ones won't.'

Charles noticed Roland's face as they watched the parade work its way down Swanston Street. The boy's eyes sparkled at the display of marching bands, magicians, dancers, roving street theatre and singing groups. A smile, affixed to his face for the duration of the event, grew even bigger when he looked up at his father and thanked him for bringing them. The boy waved his new Australian flag at the passing procession with such vigour, Charles thought his arm would ache for the rest of the day. Leslie wasn't as animated or as interested in the events but clapped enthusiastically at the singing and the bands. The girls, in awe of the costumes, the noise and the people, moved their heads from side to side trying not to miss anything. They reminded Charles of the hens in the henhouse when they heard a noise they didn't recognise; their heads jerked up from pecking the ground, and they looked anxiously from side to side until satisfied all was well. Two-year-old Doris Margaret, mesmerised by the activities, moved from one parent to the other making sure she missed nothing. Charles commented to Margaret that this was the quietest Doris had been since her birth.

Margaret arranged to meet William and Annie and their children, William Jr and Constance near the Herbarium in the Botanic Gardens. If it hadn't been for William's top hat popping out of the crowd, they would have missed each other.

Setting the food on a blanket on the ground, Margaret and Annie organised lunch for their families. The younger children played nearby while Roland helped his mother and aunt.

'Your eldest is very considerate,' William said to Charles while they strolled around the area in which the children were playing. 'He is always concerned for my sister and his siblings. What do you think the future holds for him?'

Charles knew Roland to be a caring soul but hadn't thought about the eleven-year-old's future. 'Perhaps he will go into business as you and I have done. William, while we wait for lunch, tell me about your business opportunities.'

Stopping under one of the trees that had been planted fifty years earlier, and now offered a huge shady canopy to escape the January sun, William stood straight and folded his arms across his chest. 'I am to be a partner in the silk merchant firm I have worked in since returning from London. It will be renamed Makower, McBeath & Co. and I am standing for election as a councillor in the Boroondara Shire. This is the beginning, Charles. I want to leave a legacy, I want to be remembered for doing good deeds and for making good business judgements. And I want to make lots of money. My poor Mama had little growing up when her father lost farms in Tasmania and Port Phillip. My Grandmama took in mending, sewing and dressmaking to feed her children and moved from house to house whenever the rents increased. When my parents met, my mother's lifestyle changed for the better. I want my family to have a good life that will not deteriorate if I die early like my father did.'

Charles nodded. 'Congratulations, William. I understand about the necessity of seeing your family looked after. My father left my siblings and me a tidy sum each when he died. That secured mine and Margaret's future, bought the shop and the cottage at the rear, and paid for the start of my business. They have also accepted me as a member of the Oddfellows, so, if I die early as my father did, my family too will cared for.'

The men shook hands, collected the children and sauntered back to enjoy their Federation picnic.

44

MARGARET FRANCES WERRETT (NEE MCBEATH)

1903

By a strange twist of fate, my sister-in-law Annie and I are expecting babies at the same time. It's been ten years since Annie's last child, Constance May was born. If not for my brother's extended absences travelling for business to London, New Zealand, and back to Melbourne, tongues would wag about Annie's inability to fall pregnant, or of problems with their marriage.

My brother is an ambitious and successful businessman. As a partner in Makower, McBeath & Co, he has grown the company to New Zealand, Adelaide, Sydney and Brisbane. Like our father, he doesn't rest on current achievements; he is always planning future endeavours. Now he is building a mansion in Toorak while also an elected councillor and soon to be mayor of Boroondara Shire. Annie and I can't vote for him in the Council elections because women don't have the right to vote in Victorian government or local government elections. The suffragette movement is gaining momentum however, especially since we have the right to vote, and stand for parliament in Commonwealth elections.

My husband has no interest in becoming a politician, but he

offers his premises as a polling station during elections. He is a successful businessman but lacks the relentless drive and ambition of my brother.

Charles business has expanded to where he now has employees to make shoes and boots in a workshop behind the shop. Each morning he dresses in a suit and tie, opens the shop and looks after customers all day. He bought bigger premises on Whitehorse Road and purchased a substantial home for us in Balwyn.

Annie gave birth to another little girl, Annie Elizabeth, and our third son, Norman William arrived shortly after. Norman is our sixth child and I thank God each time we have a healthy baby who survives infancy.

Our eldest child, Roland Charles is now thirteen, and even though he is still a most caring and devoted son, he displays wandering tendencies. He often returns late from school, not I believe to shirk his responsibilities at home, or to not help his father in the shop, but because he is easily distracted by events that go on around him. He investigates the neighbourhood to observe new buildings, new residents, new shops and other businesses. Charles hopes Roland will join him on Whitehorse Road when his education is complete, but I have my doubts.

Leslie Francis loves gardening as his grandfather, Richard did. Charles is proud that a part of his own father has reappeared in one of his sons. Leslie keeps to himself, does his chores, goes to school, comes home and works in the back and front gardens of our home.

Pearl and Phyllis are at school and seem to be happy. They attend my Aunt Frances' school at 76 Moray Place, South Melbourne, where my sister Ethel and I went. My Aunt has an excellent reputation in Melbourne for her school, and the curriculum she delivers. William's daughter, Constance also attends. The Jubilee History of Victoria and Melbourne, published in 1888, gave a glowing report on my Aunt's school:

"MISS F. A. BLAY,
76 Moray Place, South Melbourne, Private School for children. Established

in 1875. The increasing numbers of pupils attending this lady's school are a sufficient guarantee of its popularity and usefulness. Parents who do not care to educate their children at the expense of the State cannot do better than take advantage of Miss Blay's establishment, the curriculum of which is acknowledged to be one of the best of the kind to be found among the private schools.[1]"

Aunt Frances loves teaching and was first registered when she was fifteen. As women may now vote in Australia, my Aunt Frances told me she hopes the law will change for younger women entering the teaching profession. Frances has never married, she chose teaching over a husband and family. My daughters are growing up in a society that shows more opportunity for women, but realistically only for those who choose not to marry.

5th February 1905

On one of the hottest February days I can remember our seventh child, and fourth son, Hector Ralph Werrett joined our family. My body is sagging in areas I didn't think it would be possible to sag, and each time I give birth to a child, even though the labour seems shorter, I work harder. This infant was reluctant to leave the sanctuary of my womb and as my strength evaporated, one final push that exhausted any reserves of energy I had, brought him into the world. With his dark hair and deep brown eyes Charles commented that Hector had a serious, all-knowing look on his face. He looked as if he had been in this world before and wasn't happy coming back to it.

1906

My beloved Aunt, Frances Amy, has passed away. A tireless educator and champion of education for girls, I remember my Mama saying that Frances had the sweetest nature of any person she knew, and that her brothers and sisters loved her dearly. It is a coincidence that my middle name is the same as my aunt's, because I was named after my father, David Francis. One of Mama's older sisters, Caroline, called one of her daughters Frances Amy because she was so enamoured with Frances' personality. Although my aunt never married, or had children, the children she educated at her school would remember her fondly, forever.

Mama's siblings put a notice in the newspaper about Aunt Frances' death. I thought it telling that they left my uncle William James, and my aunt Sarah Susannah out of the notice.

"BLAY – On the 25th October, at her residence at Tope Street, South Melbourne, Frances Amy, youngest daughter of the late William and Margaret Blay; beloved sister of Mrs Bulmer, of Lake Tyers; Mrs Harding and John Douglas Blay." [2]

My oldest sister, Elizabeth Nicholson McBeath is a teacher also, and she is not married. She teaches in country Victoria and often moves to new rural schools. I am a little saddened that intelligent young women are forced to choose between a career in teaching or a husband and family. I fail to see why both are not possible.

1908 – 1912

I'm thirty-eight years old but physically I am sure my body looks as if I am one hundred and thirty-eight. However sagging and stretched my body is, I am pleased that Charles still finds me attractive. This little girl, though, I pray will be my last child. Born in 1908, Florence Winifred is our eighth child. We have four sons and four daughters. I find I am avoiding Charles in the evenings if I think he is interested in making love. I don't want any more children.

1910

Although far removed from our comfortable life on 268 Whitehorse Road, Balwyn[3], I found an interesting article in the newspaper about the death of a woman called Elizabeth Blay from Portland. Mama was Elizabeth Blay. I didn't wait for the children to come home from school. I put Florence into a jacket to protect against the horrid north wind typical of springtime, sat her in the baby carriage, tied a scarf around my hair, put a cardigan over my long-sleeved dress, and walked to the tram stop. My Aunt Maggie would know of this Elizabeth Blay in Portland.

The children waited while I had a cup of tea with my Aunt. She did know Elizabeth Blay in Portland, in fact she remembered her from when her mother and father brought her, Sarah and Caroline from Tasmania to Victoria. She said they lived in a house near Elizabeth and her husband John, who was her Papa's brother. She said her mother and Elizabeth were very fond of each other and were upset to leave each other. 'Your grandpapa took us to River Plenty and Uncle John took his family to Geelong, then Portland.'

"Death of a Pioneer

The death is announced at Portland of Mrs John Blay in her 94th year. She was a colonist since 1838. Mrs Blay was born at Government House, Hobart town on January 8, 1817, her mother being nurse to Mrs Sorell, wife of Colonel Sorell, Governor of Van Diemen's Land. Mrs Blay was christened by the Rev. Robert Knopwood.
On leaving school Mrs Blay entered the service as lady's maid of Lady Franklin, wife of Sir John Franklin, and remained there till her marriage at New Norfolk at the age of 17 years, to John Blay, son of a prosperous farmer in the New Norfolk district. They resided at Green Ponds after their marriage, and then, hearing reports of the new settlement at Melbourne, decided to go there. Leaving Hobart Town in a vessel called the Swan River Packet, they arrived at Melbourne in the latter part of 1838. They landed in

the surf near where is now Port Melbourne. With her baby in her arms, Mrs Blay was carried ashore by a sailor. Melbourne only comprised a few huts and tents, and on one of the latter the family made their home and lived for some time. Mrs Blay often related that the golden wattle was in full bloom everywhere, and that grass was abundant and fully 2ft high. She saw "Johnny" Fawkner, whom she knew well, once land from a bot after a Yarra exploration trip, and dance a hornpipe on the banks, saying with glee that this was the settlement for him.

"*Mrs Blay was present at the first land sale in 1840...Melbourne for some time experienced a period of depression, and Mr and Mrs Blay, with an increased family of five, in 1843 left for Geelong, where they stayed nearly two years, and then decided to go to Portland. The trip was taken with a bullock team, the journey occupying five weeks, Mrs Blay, with an infant two weeks old, sitting on top of the dray. They arrived in Portland in April 1845. Mrs Blay resided there continuously till her death yesterday morning, a period of 65 years. Mrs Blay had a family of 14, 11 of whom survive her, the youngest being over 50 years of age. There are also a very large number of grand and great-grandchildren. Mrs Blay for many years had the distinction of being the oldest living Australian native.*"[4]

Aunt Maggie read the article and wiped a tear from her cheek. 'I remember Mama and Aunt Elizabeth being so close. Mama was heart-broken when Aunt Elizabeth and Uncle John left for Geelong, and then Portland. When we first moved to Greenhills, we would still see them because it was only fifteen miles from Melbourne to our farm. They came to your Mama's baptism at St James' Church. The two families were close, and we children played together. Mama and Papa had all daughters, and Elizabeth and John had all sons while they were in Melbourne.'

I'll show this article to my brother. Having a family member with such a connection to the pioneer days of Victoria will delight him.

1912

Another family event that is a long way removed from us, and yet validates my brother's claim to be from a respectable background, is the golden wedding anniversary of our Aunt Caroline and her husband, John Bulmer. William showed me the article in Table Talk, a publication I don't have time to read: He said our parents met at Aunt Caroline's wedding to John Bulmer.

Golden Wedding 1912.

"A notable golden wedding was celebrated on Thursday, January 4, at Lake Tyers Aboriginal Station, Gippsland Lakes. The Rev. John Bulmer and Mrs Bulmer were married on January 4, 1862, at St Mark's Church Fitzroy, and shortly afterwards they journeyed to Lake Tyers, where Mr Bulmer took charge of the mission station, and for 45 years was its superintendent and missioner. He is still carrying out the duties of the latter position. In the early years of the mission the building up of the settlement and the care and education of the aborigines were attended with many difficulties, and Mr Bulmer was in turn builder, farmer, teacher, doctor, and pastor, and was ably aided by his wife and, in later years, by the members of his family. Mr Bulmer devoted himself to his life's work with a zeal and enthusiasm worthy of the highest praise and he and his family have won the respect and affection of their charges right through the long period of years culminating ....jubilee.

At the celebration of their jubilee on Thursday last there was great jubilation at the mission station, and the natives joined in the rejoicing in characteristic fashion. The members of the Bulmer family mustered in force and, with their wives, husbands and grand-children, numbered 25. Relatives and friends were also there. The old couple were the guests of the day, the family relieving them of all the care and preparations for the celebration. At dinner, Captain John T. Eggers, Mr Bulmer's oldest friend (of 63 years...) proposed the healths of Mr and Mrs Bulmer in most cordial and reminiscent forms. The toast was enthusiastically honored and Mr Bulmer appropri-

ately responded. After festivities took place, and a very happy and enjoyable day was spent by all. Many congratulations were received from other friends. A united presentation was made by the natives and a few personal friends of a ...of gold..."[5]

Whilst my brother gloated and preened over the report of our worthy Aunt and her husband's golden wedding anniversary, Charles received an honour that validated his passion to help others, and to be a respected member of our community. Charles is a member of the Independent Order of Oddfellows and although women are not allowed membership, he tells me some of what happens in the meetings. When he arrived home from the July meeting he proudly showed me his past officer's certificate. Our eldest son, Roland went with his father to the meeting. I think Charles hopes Roland will join the organisation.

6

45

THE FIRST WORLD WAR

First World War

"There was no single definitive factor that caused the start of the First World War. Tensions throughout Europe had been growing for many years – nationalism, an arms race, disputes over territories and spheres of influence, greed, fear, distrust, and the division of Europe into two hostile alliances were all contributing factors. The assassination of Archduke Franz Ferdinand, heir to the Austro-Hungarian throne, by Serbian terrorists led to the Austro-Hungarian invasion of Serbia, on 29 July 1914. Russia mobilised troops to prevent Serbia being crushed. Germany declared war on Russia and, realising that France would support Russia, declared war on France as well. When Germany invaded neutral Belgium, Britain declared war on Germany. Japan, seeing the chance to seize German territory in China, also declared war on Germany. Bulgaria and Turkey sided with the Central Powers and soon most countries in Europe had become involved in the war."

http://rslnsw.org.au/commemoration/heritage/the-first-world-war

"During World War 1, McBeath was a principal business adviser to the Commonwealth Department of Defence. Public pressure after some spectacular pay-embezzlement scandals, as well as obvious overspending on defence equipment, forced the Hughes government to appoint a royal commission on navy and defence administration in July 1917. McBeath was chairman, with Sydney retailer J. Chalmers and Adelaide merchant F. A. Verco the other members. Their report was presented in four parts between December 1917 and March 1918. Though recognizing the extreme stress under which the Defence Department had been operating, the report found 'muddle, waste and fraud' and 'chaos in pay offices', and drew attention to a lack of accountancy and business training. Its main recommendations, adopted by the government, involved a complete restructure of defence supply and support, removing them from military control and establishing a three-member central board of business administration. During the reorganization McBeath acted as an honorary member of this board."

Australian Dictionary of Biography, Volume 10, (MUP), 1986. Author, Margaret Vines.

1915

C harles Werrett stifled a gasp that he knew if it exited his throat, would become a cry of despair. His eldest child, Roland, stood in the kitchen of their home in Balwyn, with Australian Army enlistment papers[1] in his hand.

Charles half expected his son to join the army, but he and Margaret harboured hope their son would stay home and keep working in the family business. Pulling out a chair from the kitchen table, he sat on it more heavily than he'd intended. Pointing to the seat on the opposite side, he told Roland to sit. 'This news will devastate your mother. We both hoped you would keep your wandering spirit in check and find a wife.'

'I know, Papa, but there is nothing either of you can do to dissuade me. I believe we must defend our freedoms. I won't leave that defence to my friends while I remain here, selling shoes to well-to-do snobs who should also be fighting.'

'I'm not telling your mother, you will do that. If you are man enough to put on a uniform, hold a gun and kill another human being, you are man enough to tell your mother yourself. Please make sure you are here for supper this evening, tell her before she finds out from a gossiping neighbour.'

Watching his wife deal with the reality of their eldest son going to war, Charles wrung his hands, wiped the perspiration off his brow and took their youngest, Florence, by the hand to get her seated for the Army sanctioned family photograph. Rolie (Roland) was in his uniform, ready to take his place at the back of their group. He was a grown man, and Charles knew that if war had been declared when he was twenty-four, he would have enlisted too. Rolie had told his father that not having a wife or children to worry about had made his decision easier. His eldest was a sensible fellow and Charles prayed he would not take unnecessary risks.

Whilst watching his family take their places as directed by the photographer, a wave of relief washed over Charles as he realised Rolie would be the only son to go to this war. Leslie and his wife Ethel had a twelve-month-old son, Ronald Sidney, and Ethel was expecting again. Leslie had said he would not leave his family. The other two boys, Norman and Hector were too young.

Before he took his place on the seat as indicated by the photographer, Charles looked at Margaret. In the twenty-five-years they'd been married he had never known her face to show the anguish she felt in her heart, as it did this day. No matter how the photographer prompted, she could not bring herself to smile. To Charles, she looked as if she were calling on inner strength to fight back a flood of tears.

2

22nd Battalion AIF

"The 22nd Battalion AIF was formed on 26 March 1915 at Broadmeadows Camp in Victoria. The battalion became part of the 6th Brigade of the 2nd Division.

Most of the battalion embarked for Egypt on 8 May 1915. The battalion deployed to Gallipoli in the first week of September 1915 allowing elements of the 2nd Brigade to be rested from their positions in the front line at ANZAC. The battalion served on the peninsula until the final evacuation in December 1915, and were then withdrawn to Egypt and brought back to strength with reinforcements...

. . .

In March 1916, the battalion embarked for France and experienced their first service on the Western Front in reserve breastwork trenches near Fleurbaix at the end of the first week of April 1916. The battalion's first major action was at Pozieres, part of the massive British offensive on the Somme. In September/October they were moved to the Ypres sector then back to the Somme for the winter. The battalion spent most of 1917 bogged in bloody trench warfare from Bullecourt to Broodseinde in Flanders. In 1918 the battalion returned to the Somme valley. After helping to stop the German spring offensive in March and April, the 6th Brigade participated in the period of peaceful penetration of the enemy lines. It was in mid-May that Sergeant William 'Rusty' Ruthven earned the 22nd Battalion's only Victoria Cross. In the last days of August and September the battalion helped capture Mont St Quentin. The 22nd Battalion took part in the last action fought by the AIF on the Western Front, the battle of Montbrehain, in October 1918.

At 11 am on 11 November 1918 the guns on the Western Front fell silent. The November Armistice was followed by the Peace Treaty of Versailles signed on 28 June 1919. The last elements of the battalion began their journey home from the Western Front in May 1919 to return to Australia for demobilisation and discharge.[3]"

46

MARGARET FRANCES WERRETT

1915

We went to Station Pier on 28 June to see Rolie off on the transport ship *Berrima* He was going to Egypt. Charles stood back and let me hug our son until my tears soaked the shoulder of his uniform. When I stepped away, Rolie quickly wiped his cheek.

'I'll be fine, Mama. You look after yourself and Hector and Florence and be a good grandmother to Leslie and Ethel's children.'

Picking up his pack and throwing it over his shoulder, our grown-up son shook hands with his father, gave me one last kiss on the cheek, bent down and kissed Florence, shook the hands of his brothers, and left to join his battalion.

Eight months after they shipped my eldest child off to the other side of the world to fight a battle that isn't his, my daughter-in-law gave birth to another baby boy. Leslie and Ethel named the child Francis Roland. I'm thrilled to have my father remembered in this child's name, and to have Rolie's bravery acknowledged.

1917

Life is going on without Rolie. Charles is running his business as usual, the younger children, Norman, Hector and Florence are in school. Pearl is seeing a man called Charles Christopher Thiel, Phyllis' beau, Ronald Robert Williams, has gone to war, and Phyllis promised him she would wait for him. I pray her waiting won't be in vain. Doris is helping me with the house and keeping the books in her father's shop. Leslie and his wife Ethel have another boy, Sydney Herbert Werrett, born on 10 May. Charles and I have three grandsons.

We are fortunate that the War is so far from our shores. The newspapers are full of stories and photographs each day of the bombing of London, and the other horrors of the theatre of war. Most nights, as I lay in bed before I go to sleep, I try to bury the feelings of guilt that plague every waking moment. As we live our lives with some inconveniences, our son and other sons like him, are fighting, being injured, and dying far away from home.

My brother, William, is a principal advisor to the Commonwealth Department of Defence. His star is rising in business and government. He is a friend of the Prime Minister, Billy Hughes, and has been appointed Chairman of the Royal Commission on Navy and Defence Administration. [1] My nephew, William George, although the same age as Rolie, chose not to enlist. I try to be generous in my estimation of my nephew, because Leslie is of the age to enlist, and he also chose not to. William George is the only son of my brother and his wife, Annie, so I understand my brother's reluctance to see his son go to war.

While Rolie is fighting in France, I am busy with the Red Cross Society, organising packages to send overseas to the soldiers. Charles cuts out the newspaper articles each time they mention my name in one. I would rather he didn't. It's not recognition we mothers want, it's our sons to return home alive.

1918

Charles came into the living room after work, with a copy of *The Argus* under his arm. Opening it up to page 8, he put it on my lap and pointed to an article that mentioned Rolie.

'Our son is cited for conspicuous service,' he said, 'It confirms the letter I received from the AIF saying he was mentioned in despatches.'

"WERRETT – Mr and Mrs C Werrett, of Balwyn, have received word that their son, Company Sergeant Major R. Werrett, has been mentioned in despatches for conspicuous services by Sir Douglas Haig. He enlisted in March, 1915, and saw service at Gallipoli, being amongst those first to land in France." [2]

I smiled at my husband, pride layering his face like icing on a cake. But I wanted to scream at him that I don't want my son taking risks and being mentioned for conspicuous service. I want him to keep his head down and come home in one piece. Instead, I asked 'How will you find out what he did?'

'I'll call *The Argus* tomorrow to see if they know anything else. And I'm going to write to your brother, William, to see if he can find out any more.'

1919

The guns fell silent on what they are calling the First World War, on 11th November, 1918, but Rolie still isn't home. He went to Egypt, fought at Gallipoli and the Somme, went back to London when he was sick, and then back to France. Surely he has completed his service. I ache to see him.

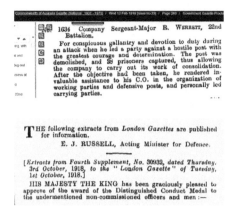

Commonwealth of Australia Gazette (National 1901 - 1973) / Wed 12 Feb 1919 [Issue No.20] / Page 260 / Government Gazette Procla

1634 Company Sergeant-Major R. WERRETT, 22nd Battalion.

For conspicuous gallantry and devotion to duty during an attack when he led a party against a hostile post with the greatest courage and determination. The post was demolished, and 29 prisoners captured, thus allowing the company to carry out its work of consolidation. After the objective had been taken, he rendered invaluable assistance to his C.O. in the organization of working parties and defensive posts, and personally led carrying parties.

THE following extracts from *London Gazettes* are published for information.

E. J. RUSSELL, Acting Minister for Defence.

[*Extracts from Fourth Supplement, No. 30932, dated Thursday, 3rd October, 1918, to the " London Gazette " of Tuesday, 1st October, 1918.*]

HIS MAJESTY THE KING has been graciously pleased to approve of the award of the Distinguished Conduct Medal to the undermentioned non-commissioned officers and men :—

3

Finally we received word from the AIF that Rolie was on his way home. He left London on the *Castalia* on 13 April 1919. The process of bringing the soldiers home has been drawn out and created much anxiety with those of us waiting for our sons, and sometimes our daughters, to return. Whilst Rolie has been away, his brother Leslie and his wife, Ethel have had two more children: Sydney Herbert, and Eunice May. Pearl has married Charles Thiel, Phyllis is still waiting for Ronald Williams, who, thank God, survived the War. Doris is twenty and working in a shop near her father's business in Whitehorse Road. Hector is fifteen and almost finished school,

Norman is seventeen and an apprentice builder. Florence is eleven and still attending school.

Rolie trudged off the ship with the other men in his battalion. When he left four years ago, he was twenty-four-years-old excited to see the world and defend his country from the threats the politicians convinced us existed. Charles and I wait patiently. We have waited four years, we can wait a few more minutes. He is coming; he is alive.

The rest of the family is at home putting up decorations and getting food ready for a welcome home lunch for our soldier.

Throwing his pack on the ground, Rolie put his arms around me, and lifted me in a hug that almost crushed my ribs. 'Hi Mum,' he said through a grin that took up half of his face. 'Hi Dad,' he said, holding out his hand to shake with his father. A handshake wasn't enough for Charles, he stepped towards his son and held him in an embrace until Rolie laughed that people were gawking.

'Where is everyone?' Rolie asked.

'At home, waiting for you. The girls are preparing lunch and Hector and Florence and Leslie's children are putting up decorations. It's a surprise,' I said to Rolie, winking.

Picking up his pack and tossing it back over his shoulder, our decorated soldier son, walked with us to get a taxi home. His lined face showed an age much older than twenty-eight. His hair had grey streaks, his scarred hands and gnarled fingers gave the impression of a lifetime of work. His uniform hung on his frame, too big for him. He'd folded the sleeves back, and his belt was pulled in tight to keep his trousers up.

'I'm looking forward to wearing a pair of shoes that fit properly, Dad,' he said to Charles as the taxi driver held the door open for us to get into his vehicle.

'Where did Mum and Dad come from?' I asked as we settled into the car.

'That's what the English call their parents. No-one says Mama and Papa anymore, Mum, it's the twentieth century.'

'You can call us whatever you wish, Rolie,' Charles said to him.

'Before we get home and I get swamped by everyone and answer questions until my mouth dries up, I met a girl in France. Her name is Claire. I proposed to her and I'll be going back to France to marry her.'

'That's lovely, Rolie,' I said, holding back the anger that would tell him he just got home and now he was talking about going away again. 'Will you stay in France?'

'We haven't decided, Mum. She wants to come to Australia to see if she likes it. We'll work it out when the time comes.'

Charles looked at me and shook his head. I knew he was telling me to be quiet, not to say anymore, to let Rolie have his welcome home, and to worry about him returning to France another day. Charles was right. I would wait.

My brother has more achievements to add to his impressive list. He was awarded a Commander of the British Empire during the last year of the war, and in 1918 they appointed him Chairman of the State Savings Bank of Victoria. He told Charles and I that he wanted to lead the Bank into the future while helping customers achieve their goals. As the war ended the Prime Minister appointed my brother Financial Advisor to the Commonwealth for the demobilization of the Australian Imperial Force, of which Rolie was a part. William is going to London where he will take on the role of Chairman of the AIF Disposals Board. Annie and the children will go with him, not knowing how long the work will take to complete. During the War we didn't see as much of William and Annie as in the past. My brother was very busy working for the Commonwealth, and Annie was busy with social activities and the war effort. Our worlds are far apart.

47

<hr/>

CHARLES MARK WERRETT

1920

Rolie opened the door of his father's shop in Whitehorse Road and as he closed it, waited for the bell that hung on the door to stop tinkling. Looking up, the sight of his eldest son chased away the frown that had been on Charles' forehead and replaced it with raised eyebrows and a grin.

'Nice to see you, Dad,' Rolie said.

'You too, my boy. But you have come for a reason, not just to see my rugged handsome face.'

Rolie smiled at his father's attempt to lighten the mood. 'I've booked passage to France, I'm leaving next month.' [1]

'I hope this girl is worth it, Rolie.'

Charles didn't tell Margaret about Rolie's announcement until they were in bed and the house was quiet. He didn't want to alarm Hector and Florence. Their older brother had been brought back to them in one piece from battlefields on the other side of the world. The prospect of him wanting to return to those battlefields was difficult for them. Neither understood why Rolie would want to go all the way back to France for a girl.

When Charles finished telling Margaret about Rolie's visit to the shop, and the news he shared, Margaret turned away from him and curled herself into such a small ball that Charles thought she'd sunk into the bed. He let her cry in peace.

For the second time in five years, Charles and Margaret stood on the dock and waved goodbye to their eldest son. This time, as he waved and blew kisses, he was smiling and wearing a beautifully cut suit, perfectly fitting shoes his father had made for him, and a fashionable hat. Margaret and Charles stood on the dock until the *Commonwealth* sailed into Port Phillip Bay and they could no longer see their son.

Charles picked up Margaret's hand and held it in his as they walked to the tram stop. He wanted to reassure her that not everything in their lives would change. 'I love you,' he told her.

'I love you too, Charles. Very much. Oh, and something completely irrelevant to our son leaving again and you and I loving each other, my brother has been invested a Knight of the British Empire. So you and I will call him Sir William and my sister-in-law Lady Annie from now on.'

Charles pulled Margaret into him, said he didn't care, and kissed her, not worrying whether it was an appropriate act for public display, or how many people tut tutted on their way past.

1921

Charles paced while Margaret fussed over her appearance. She had changed her dress three times, put on two different hats, and asked him if she needed a coat at least five times.

Hector and Florence waited in the living room for their parents. Hector fidgeted with his tie, looked in the mirror over the mantelpiece to check that his hair was in place, walked to the washhouse for a rag to polish his shiny new shoes that his father had made, washed and dried his hands and ran his fingers down the front of his jacket to make sure every button was secured.

'Stop it,' wailed Florence to Hector. 'You are driving me mad. We are not going to collect the King from Port Melbourne, we are collecting our brother. Why do you always have to check and double check that you look perfect?'

'He is our older brother. He has been to war and gone back to France. Now he is coming home with a French bride. I've missed him. I want to look my best.' Hector retaliated.

'Stop fighting,' Charles ordered when he walked into the room. 'Your mother will be here in a moment, and then we'll leave. I've booked a taxi. I don't want our French daughter-in-law having to catch a tram home.'

'Why can't she get a tram?' Florence demanded. 'We manage.'

'Don't be insolent, Florence. I want her to have a good first impression. She is French after all.'

Florence screwed up her face, sat further back on the couch, crossed her legs and folder her arms over her chest.

'What are you sulking about?' Margaret asked coming into the room.

2

'Nothing, she's not sulking about anything,' Charles said. 'Let's get going or we'll be late.'

. . .

Rolie was a tall man and the first thing Charles noticed about his son's new bride was her height. She stood as tall as Rolie with a straight posture to match her husband's. They walked off the ship arm in arm. Rolie waved to his family, patted his wife's hand and pointed to his parents and siblings.

Hector ran to greet his older brother, stopping himself from throwing his arms around him, Hector held out his hand. Rolie took it and then pulled him in for a hug.

'Hector, this is my wife, Claire. Claire, this is my youngest brother, Hector.'

Claire bent down and kissed Hector on one cheek and then the other. 'Bonjour,' she said.

Charles could see the colour run to Hector's face as this exotic French woman greeted him. 'Hector is in awe already,' he said to Margaret.

Introductions complete and luggage collected, Charles led the group to a small café on the end of Station Pier. He watched as Rolie pulled out a chair for his mother, and then his wife, making sure the women were sitting next to each other. Hector's face was still red, and Florence was staring at her new sister-in-law.

'I've been teaching Claire English, and she is teaching me French,' Rolie told his family.

Claire nodded and smiled at Margaret. 'It is nice to meet you,' the young woman said slowly and with purpose.'

'And it is nice to meet you, Claire,' Margaret answered.

'Indeed,' added Charles.

3

chison. June 10, 1889. One son and two daughters. Clubs: Melbourne, Australian, Yorick, Royal Melbourne and Royal Sydney Golf (Victoria), Devonshire (London). Recreations: Golf and tennis. Creed: Presbyterian. Home address: Irving Road, Toorak. Country residence: Mt. Macedon, Victoria.

McBEATH, Sir William George,
K.B.E., J.P., Makower, McBeath and
Co. Pty. Ltd., Merchants. 230 Flinders
Lane, Melbourne, Victoria. Established
1890. Chairman of Directors, Makower,
McBeath and Co. Pty. Ltd. and the
Bankers and Traders Insurance Co., Vic-
toria; Chairman of Commissioners State
Savings Bank; President of National Union.
Born Fitzroy, Victoria, 1865. Son of
David Francis McBeath, of Belfast, Ireland,
and Elizabeth McBeath, of Fitzroy, Mel-
bourne. Educated Nelson College. Has
been a member of the Camberwell City
Council for 27 years; elected Mayor five
times; retired 1918. Chairman of Royal
Commission on Navy and Defence De-
partments 1916-18; member of Business
Board, Defence Department, 1916-18;
Chairman of Australian Imperial Force Disposals' Board, London, 1919-20; Financial Adviser, A.I.F., London, 1919; member of Board of Trustees War Relief Fund;
Australian Delegate, 5th Assembly, League
of Nations, Geneva, 1924. Married Annie
McHutchison, daughter of Duncan McHut-

48

MARGARET FRANCES WERRETT (NEE MCBEATH)

1922

A t 6.30 Hector, already shaved and hair combed, came into the kitchen for breakfast. He starts his first full-time position today. Since leaving school he has been managing the books for Charles' shoe business but after speaking with my brother one day over lunch, he was offered a position at Makower McBeath, where William is Managing Director. Hector will work in the offices in Flinders Lane. Charles isn't comfortable with Hector's decision, he doesn't want to be seen to exploit the generosity of his brother-in-law, but William insists that's what families do.

While he waits for me to finish preparing his breakfast, Hector's repetitive behaviours, that are exacerbated when he's anxious, occupy his attention. He straightens the knife and fork, moves the napkin from the right side of his place setting to the left, moves his glass to the centre of the setting, and rolls the sleeves of his dressing gown up past his elbows. The dressing gown action is new, I'll watch to see if he does it tomorrow. If so he has added another action to his repeated steps. My youngest child, Florrie, scolds Hector for his idiosyncrasies which makes him worse.

Hector has allowed twenty minutes for his breakfast, from 6.30 to 6.50 am. His timetable then allocates thirty minutes, from 6.50 until 7.20 to get dressed for work. He will leave the house at 7.25 am for the 7.34 train to the city, arriving at work at 7.50 for an 8.00 am start. Three days last week he went through the timetable making sure he allowed enough time to complete his tasks. Charles worries about him, but at least he is predictable and dependable.

After four weeks working at Makower McBeath & Co., Hector rushed in to the house one afternoon, waving the Argus around in the air. 'Mum, Uncle William's company has given money to the Great Ocean Road Scheme. They do so much good for the community.'

Hector sat down at the kitchen table and opened the page of the paper for me to see. 'Fifty pounds doesn't seem that much for a wealthy company like Uncle William's,' I said after reading the short piece.

'Mum,' Hector growled. 'They didn't' have to give anything.'

The social pages in today's *Australasian* have told all of Melbourne that my brother and sister-in-law and their two daughters, Constance and Annie have gone to Sydney for a short holiday.[1] Charles is becoming annoyed by what he sees as petty attention given to people of wealth in this city. He argues that the social divide his parents freed themselves of when they left England, has manifested itself on our side of the world.

One of my brother's contributions to this expanding city of Melbourne is to champion free kindergartens. As financial advisor to the Free Kindergarten Union, he applied pressure to the Premier for increased funds, and they increased the grant from £1,000 to £1,500.[2] These achievements make me proud. But not as proud as Hector, who cuts out each newspaper article that mentions my brother and sticks it in a note book.

1923

Rolie and Claire have a beautiful little boy. They called him *Hubert*, but we'll be saying *Herbert*, or *Herbie* when we speak to the child. Claire's English has improved. We can now have a good conversation. She's been reading the newspapers to teach herself. Rolie is still learning French, he has a French dictionary and goes to the library to borrow French novels. My secret fear is that he intends to return to France. Otherwise why does he need to speak French?

1924

The postman knocked on the door with the letter. He'd noticed a New Zealand postmark and thought he'd hand deliver it instead of putting it in the mailbox. Thanking him, I closed the door, and turned the envelope over and over as I made my way to the kitchen table. It was from my younger sister, Ethel. She didn't write often; I was hesitant to open it in case it brought bad news. Using a butter knife from the kitchen drawer, I slid it under the fold of the envelope and swept it along the crease. Ethel always had a beautiful hand, I could see her writing through the sheets of folded paper.

My dearest sister, Margaret

It is with great excitement that I write to inform you that I am married. Yes, at the age of fifty! Better late than never!

My husband is Hector Finch McKay. He is fifty-eight and has been married before. His first wife died in 1917. Hector was born in New Zealand and is interested in going to Australia. We might be coming home, Margaret.

I will keep you informed.

All my love, your sister, Ethel McKay.

My hands stopped shaking, it was good news. I couldn't be happier for Ethel. She and I attended our Aunt Frances' school in South Melbourne together, and when she was old enough, she went back to New Zealand to live with our father's family in Nelson. She was managing one of the drapery stores the McBeath's ran and whenever she wrote; it was to say she was happy and busy. A husband, that's wonderful.

Hector arrived home from work and sat down at the kitchen table with the *Australasian* newspaper open in front of him. The piece he cut out told the public that "The Chairman of the State Savings Bank (Sir William McBeath) left Melbourne by the *Narkunda* for Europe on a health journey and will be absent for eight or nine months." [3]

'Is there any other news in the paper, Hector?' I asked.

'About Uncle William?' he queried.

'No, Hector, about anything else.'

He shrugged, applied glue to the back of the little cutting, and stuck it on a clean page in his notebook.

1925

Hector is twenty and becoming restless. His repetitive behaviours are more numerous. He seems to add a new one every week. It's difficult to ask him if anything is troubling him because, unlike his father, and unlike my brother, he is reluctant to share concerns. I remember Grandmama lamenting that Grandpapa kept worries to himself. She said if he had shared she may have been able to help. Perhaps they could have kept the farm in Tasmania or Greenhills. Grandmama spoke too of Grandpapa William's odd behaviours. It seems my youngest son has inherited them.

'Uncle William is retiring from his position as Chairman of Makower McBeath,' Hector announced one evening after supper. I noticed he waited until Charles had moved into the living room. 'His son, our cousin, will take his place. I am not predisposed to work there with my cousin in charge. I'm looking for another position.'

I wanted to reach out, put my arms around my youngest son and hug him until his concerns seeped from his mind. Instead, I commented 'You know what is best for you, Hector. Don't stay working for my brother's company if you don't want to.'

A position found as a book-keeper at Model Dairy in Kew, Hector was in the kitchen at 6am on his first day, allowing time to complete his routine and catch the tram for the twenty-minute trip from our home to his place of employment. I didn't watch to see if any new steps crept into his routine.

1926

Roland and Claire have had another son, Pierre. Of course we'll call him Peter. And Hector has met a girl. My brother invited Charles and me, Hector and Florrie to his summer house at Mt Macedon for a weekend. William and Annie held a garden party to which the girl was also a guest. The young lady is a first cousin twice removed of the current Victorian Premier, John Allan. Her name is Alice Alexandra Proctor. Her mother, Jean Mary (nee Allan) is where the connection to the Premier fits. Hector is besotted.

4

1929

Holding Alice's hand as he sauntered into the living room, Hector announced they were getting married. With a smile so broad I thought I could count all the teeth in his mouth, Charles jumped out of his chair and hugged his youngest son until Hector complained and pushed him away. Beckoning me to get off the couch to join him, he kissed Alice on the cheek and welcomed her to the family. Stepping forward, I put my arms around my soon to be daughter-in-law and hugged her.

'Thank you,' Alice whispered.

This wasn't the time to warn Alice of Hector's idiosyncrasies. She would find out in due course.

As we prepare to welcome a new daughter-in-law into our family, one is saying goodbye. Roland, Claire, Hubert and Pierre are going to France.

49

HECTOR RALPH WERRETT

The Great Depression

"The impact of the Great Depression in Australia was considerable in the period from 1929 onwards. Whilst it is clear that the Depression was not a "sudden rupture" in events but rather part of a worsening economic trough that had its origins in the early 1890's, the Depression certainly

accentuated and intensified several problems. Unemployment

statistics for Australia in the Depression years underestimated the extent of the severity of the problem: from mid-1930 until the last months of 1934, approximately one-fifth of all wage and salary earners were out of work, and in 1932-33 almost two-thirds of all breadwinners were receiving an income of less than the basic wage. Under such conditions we might assume that a large majority of Australians experienced suffering and deprivation in this period; unable to make ends meet, and unable to find any job security for the preservation of families and individuals alike."
http://thecud.com.au/live/content/cud-history-%E2%80%94-looking-back-great-depression-australia

H ector put on the kettle to make a cup of tea for his mother. His father had already left for the shop, but he would close at lunch time: it was a Saturday. Alice and Hector were getting married the next day. Opening the notebook he'd used to keep newspaper cuttings about his Uncle William, Hector rifled through the loose cuttings he hadn't yet stuck into the book. Putting them in date order, he was sticking them when his mother came into the kitchen.

'What are you doing, Hector? I thought you'd finished following your Uncle's pursuits and recording them in your notebook.'

'I kept cutting them out, but not sticking them in the book. This is the last time I'll do it, and because Uncle William is so unwell with emphysema, I thought it might cheer him up. I'll give it to him at the wedding tomorrow.'

While his mother made a pot of tea and sliced some bread to toast for herself and her son, Hector put the cuttings into his book. [1]

Sunday 23 March 1930

Hector tried to stay in bed, tried to relax, tried not go over the day's coming events in his head. It was a futile activity. At 7am he got out of bed, put his slippers on, pulled on a summer weight dressing gown and made his way through the garden to the outhouse. It was light enough to see where he was going, and to see if there were any spiders lurking around the toilet waiting to bite him and ruin his day. Returning to the house, he went to the bathroom to wash his hands and face and to comb his receding hair.

Closing the kitchen door behind him to let his parents, and sister Florrie, sleep in, he put the kettle on for a pot of tea. The hot, sweet tea soothed his nerves a little, and he allowed himself a moment to look forward to the day. Today, he was to marry Alice. Although Uncle William didn't approve of Alice's cousin's politics (John Allan had been Premier from 1924 to 1927) the two had worked together in the Victorian Parliament and overcame many obstacles to get the Spencer Street Bridge construction back on track. Hector hoped his Uncle William was well enough to attend the wedding.

Hector's brothers Leslie and Norman were in his wedding party. Alice's attendants were her sisters, Jessie and Helen, although everyone called her *Nellie*. Jessie's daughter Marie would be flower girl.

When his mother came into the kitchen Hector had the steps for the day planned and in order. 'I'm going to my room to make sure I arrange my clothes. Yes, Mother, again. Please let me know when you and Dad are going to have breakfast. I'd like to eat something although the nerves in my stomach are playing havoc with my constitution.'

Leaving his mother to watch his back as he left the kitchen, Hector looked over his shoulder and winked at her. 'I will be fine Mum,' he said.

Standing at the altar at St Barnabas Church in Balwyn with his brothers, Hector fidgeted with the buttons on his suit jacket, played with the flower in his lapel, straightened his tie and looked at his shoes to see if they were still shiny. Florrie, watching in the family pew, hissed at Hector to stop. By the time Alice walked down the aisle on her father, Richard Proctor's arm, Hector was exhausted. As the music played, he looked up at his bride marvelling at how beautiful she looked. He marvelled even more when he remembered she had made the exquisite gown she wore, and the dresses of her sisters and niece. Alice worked as a dressmaker at Myer and would stay there until they had their first child.

Grinning, Hector took Alice's hand and turned to face the minister. Noticing as he did that his Uncle William and Aunt Annie were sitting with his parents.

1930

'I secured the housing loan,' Hector told Alice when they were curled up in the bedroom his parents had set aside for them. 'The State Savings Bank gave me the loan, and I didn't have to ask Uncle William for any help.' Alice was having a baby, and Hector wanted his family to have a place of their own.

'Have you told your parents?' Alice asked. She knew his mother would love for them to stay in this large house in Balwyn.

'No. The Bank approved the house at Wattle Avenue, Burwood. We won't be far away. Settlement is September.'

Alice and Hector had been in their new home three months when Hector's days at work were cut from five to two and a half. 'The manager said if we all cut our hours we all keep our job. If he gives some five days, then more will be put off. I don't think I can meet the mortgage payments on that money.'

Alice took in a deep breath and released it slowly. 'What will happen? The baby is due after Christmas. I don't want to move back in with your parents.'

Charles had retired but he and Margaret had substantial savings from the sale of the shoe shop in Whitehorse Road. Inviting Hector to their home for a beer one afternoon, Charles offered to lend his son money to make his mortgage payments. 'Thanks, Dad. But I can't take it. It will put you in an awkward position if any of my brothers and sisters need financial help. You won't have enough to go around, or any left for you and Mum.'

On the pretence of bringing some freshly baked biscuits into the living room for her son and husband, Margaret had dallied at the door and listened to the conversation. When she put the biscuits on the coffee table, Charles told her Hector had rejected their offer of a loan.

'I understand,' she said, 'but there is another option: you could ask your Uncle William if there is anything the bank can do to help until you are working full time again.'

1931

Hector had refused the help offered by his parents and refused to approach his uncle. As Alice went into labour with the birth of her first child, the Bank foreclosed on the house in Wattle Avenue, Burwood.

Her first child, a girl, was stillborn. Alice didn't get a chance to hold her little baby, to kiss her soft skin, to cuddle her for the first and last time. The infant was taken from her sight as quickly as the Bank had changed the locks on the doors of her home. 'I'm going to think of her as Mary,' Alice told Hector when he sat beside her bed, wiping his eyes.

Hector found them a home to rent at 14 Churchill Grove, Hawthorn. Alice came home from hospital to this house, without her baby, and without ownership of the home she would live in. Hector's obsessive habits increased in number as he came to terms with the consequences of the decisions he had made.

His beloved Uncle William died on 2nd April 1931, one month after the birth and death of his and Alice's daughter. In the space of a year, Hector's life shattered into millions of heart-broken pieces.

January 1932

With the country recovering from the Depression, the New Year started with Hector's work days being reinstated to five. Alice was heavily pregnant with their second child and bristling with anxiety as the day of her confinement grew close.

Jeanette Patricia Werrett arrived on 1st February 1932; healthy, crying loudly, her face screwed up in indignation and her little fists clenched. She was perfect.

When permitted into the room to see his wife and daughter, the relief trickled from Hector's eyes, down his cheeks onto his perfectly pressed shirt. He didn't try to stop them or wipe them away.

This day marked the opportunity for a new beginning, he told Alice. In the future, he would swallow his pride, take advice from others, and work hard to buy them another house of their own.

THE END

IS JUST BEGINNING

50

SIR WILLIAM GEORGE MCBEATH

1

- *The Geelong Advertiser, 13 June 1925*

... "*The Interstate Taxation Committee, with Sir William McBeath as its first chairman ...*"[2]

- *The Australasian, 5 September 1926* [3]

MCC Trustees.
"*Sir William McBeath was appointed a trustee of the Melbourne cricket ground site,...at a meeting of the State Executive Council on August 31...*

- *The Prahran Telegraph, 13 November 1925*

"A committee recommendation adopted by Prahran Council was that the offer of Sir William McBeath to present to this Council the land at the corner of Albany and Irving roads be accepted, and the intersection rounded off." [4]

- *The Herald 25 November 1925* [5]

"Answering the objections of the shipping interests to a fixed bridge, the Chairman of the Bridge Commission [Spencer Street Bridge, Melbourne], Sir William McBeath, said today that the commission was unanimously in favour of a fixed bridge owing to the anticipated heavy and continuous traffic."

- *The Australasian 21 May 1927.*

"Children's Hospital
Gift by Sir W. McBeath

By a gift of £2,500 Sir William McBeath and his son, Mr W.G. McBeath, have become the donors of the operating and x-ray block which will form a part of the heliotherapy branch of the Children's Hospital at

Frankston. They have requested that the buildings be called the 'Marion Nancy McBeath Block' as a memorial to the late Marion Nancy McBeath, grandchild of Sir William McBeath and daughter of Mr W.G. McBeath."[6]

7

Sir William McBeath said this marked a new era in town planning. Every man should possess his own home, it made for stability. People took more interest in Government and finance when they felt themselves a part of the counter. These houses, quite a new feature in Victoria, were the result of the manager's trip abroad. Of the 72 houses erected, 58 were already sold. The first were intended for the people of Port Melbourne who could not find homes. When this demand was satisfied, houses would be available for people in all the suburbs. Altogether there were 3500 acres at Fishermen's Bend. It was intended to make this into a garden city. The commissioners had acquired 40 acres at a cost of £13,000, and hoped to get another 340. At £5 per foot it was too dear. He hoped the Government would be more generous with the remainder of the land. What had been of Makower, McBeath, and Co. Pty. Ltd., was appointed managing director.

Sir William McBeath's wide experience and his great ability were utilised by Governments on numerous occasions. He was a tower of strength in many and varied activities. Sir William McBeath married in 1899 Miss Annie McHutchison, of Stirling, Scotland. Lady McBeath survives him, and he leaves a son (Mr. W. G. McBeath) and two daughters (Miss C. McBeath and Mrs. J. F. Williams, of Clendon road, Toorak).

The remains were cremated on Thursday afternoon.

The Australasian (Melbourne, Vic. : 1864 - 1946) / Sat 4 Apr 1931 / Page 9 / SIR WILLIAM McBEATH

DEATH ANNOUNCED.

We regret to announce that the death occurred early on Thursday morning of Sir William McBeath, of Enlinga, Irving road, Toorak.

Sir William McBeath was born at Fitzroy, Melbourne, on April 17, 1865. He was the son of Mr. David Francis McBeath, of Belfast, and he was educated at Nelson College (N.Z.). It was as a commercial traveller that he first became known in Flinders lane, but he took early steps to establish himself in business. Making a journey to Great Britain with the object of obtaining Melbourne agencies, he met on shipboard the head of the firm of Makower and Co., silk merchants, of Cheapside, London, and about 1890 he became its Melbourne agent. A few years later a member of the Makower family visiting Melbourne was so impressed by the progress which had been made in the business in Flinders lane that he opened a Melbourne branch of the company under the management of Mr. McBeath, who later became a partner and finally, when the business became a proprietary company, under its present name

8

AUTHOR'S NOTES

Information on extended family.

Betsy Pearce (nee Cullen) died in Murgheboluc, Hamilton Highway, Victoria (Golden Plains Shire) at her son James' property on 14 October 1885.

Sarah (Sadie) McMurray (nee Tedder) died in 1899 at the age of 79, in Tasmania.

William Blay and Margaret Tedder's children.

Sarah Susanna Briggs (nee Blay) died in Sydney on 5 June 1904 aged 60. She and Thomas Rowley Briggs had ten children.

Caroline Bulmer (nee Blay) died on 2 July 1918 at Lake Tyers, Gippsland, Victoria. She and John Bulmer had ten children.

John Douglas Blay died on 1st April 1915 at Lake Tyers, Gippsland, Victoria. He and his wife Elizabeth Kirby had four children.

Margaret Harding (nee Blay) (Maggie) died on 2nd August 1916. She had no children.

William James Blay. (I cannot find a death certificate that I can be certain is his. John Blay Sr and Elizabeth Fogarty also had a son called William James Blay. Grandchildren also had the same name.) William and Elizabeth Jane Welch had three children. The first, William James, died around one year of age.

———

Susanna Dwyer (nee Blay) daughter of James Blay Jr and Catherine Cullen, had three children with Edward Lovell Dwyer. She died on 27 August 1894 at age 55. She spent two months in prison from September 1841, under the name Elizabeth Dwyer.

Other children of Elizabeth Blay and David Francis McBeath.

- Elizabeth Nicholson McBeath worked as a teacher all her working life (never marrying). She died in Guildford, Victoria on 22 December 1927.
- Lilian Crosbie McBeath died in Melbourne in 1939. She never married.
- David Francis McBeath died in Bendigo, Victoria in 1941. I can find no record of a marriage.
- Ethel McBeath died in Camberwell, Victoria on 26 January 1954. She and her husband, Hector Finch McKay had no children.

Children of Charles Mark Werrett and Margaret Frances McBeath

- Hector Ralph Werrett and Alice Alexandra Proctor had three daughters. This book is dedicated to them.
- Roland Charles Werrett stayed in France with Claire and Hubert and Pierre. He died in 1976. He was made an Honorary Citizen of France. He served in the French armed forces in the Second World War. His granddaughter, Catherine, daughter of Hubert is in contact with the author.
- Leslie Francis Werrett and Ethel May Smith had three sons and one daughter. Leslie died on 10 February 1964 in Croydon, Victoria.
- Pearl Ethel Lilian Werrett married Charles Christopher Thiel. They had two sons. She died in Albury, NSW in 1981.
- Phyllis Elizabeth Werrett married Ronald Robert William Williams. They had one child. Phyllis died 12 October 1985, at Box Hill, Victoria, Australia.
- Doris Margaret married Nestor Roth. They had one child, Elizabeth. Doris died on 28 May 1977 at Ferntree Gully, Victoria, Australia.
- Norman William Werrett married Kathleen Alice Moore. They had two sons. The first, Malcolm William died at age

5. Norman died on 28 November 1955 at Canterbury, Victoria.

- Florence (Florrie) Winifred Werrett married Harmann James Webb. I think they had four children. Florence died in Balwyn, Victoria, in 1980.

Florence Louisa Werrett – daughter of Richard Werrett and Mary Ann Williams, married Arthur Ratten. Their great-grandson, Leith Ratten (1938-2012) was infamously charged with murdering his wife in 1970.

"Man dies still denying murder
Keith Moor, HeraldSun
February 3, 2012
THE man at the centre of one of the most controversial murder cases in Victorian history has died maintaining his innocence.
Family members also remained convinced Leith Ratten was wrongly convicted in 1970 over the shooting death of his pregnant wife Bev in the kitchen of their Echuca home.
Ratten died late last month in Brisbane at 73.
His brother, Graeme, 84, said Ratten should never have been jailed and claimed Bev Ratten was killed when Ratten's shotgun accidentally discharged while he was cleaning it.
A death notice in the *Herald Sun* this week referred to Ratten as the "loved husband of Bev".
What it didn't say was that Ratten was sentenced to death by a Supreme Court jury in Shepparton in 1970 for the murder of his wife, eight months pregnant with the couple's fourth child when she was shot.
Or that in rejecting an appeal to the High Court by Ratten in 1974, the then Chief Justice, Sir Garfield Barwick, said the case against Ratten was very strong and there was evidence he meant to shoot his wife.
"There was ample motive for the pressure on that trigger to have been deliberate," the High Court judgment said.
"The applicant was infatuated with another woman to the point that

he had agreed on her pressing suggestion to leave his wife and children and set up house with her."

Ratten's death sentence was commuted to 25 years, but he was released in 1983 after serving 13.

Barrister Tom Molomby, SC, and politician Don Chipp were among many who campaigned for years for Ratten's freedom.

Mr Molomby wrote a book called Ratten, subtitled, "The Web of Circumstances: how an innocent man was found guilty of murder".

Greame Ratten this week said his brother had found love again after moving to Queensland and was survived by his partner, Sandi...

Ratten ran the prison radio station 3NP in Pentridge and appeared in The Herald in 1981 with entertainer Ernie Sigley."

From left to right:

Norma Ann Lanning (nee Werrett), Elaine Joan Sullivan (nee Werrett) Alice Alexandra Werrett (nee Proctor), Jeanette Patricia Campbell (nee Werrett) Hector Ralph Werrett.

I sincerely hope you enjoyed reading the three books of the Cullen/Bartlett Dynasty.

From that First Fleet convict, transported in 1787 to the other side of the world, the generations flourished and expanded.

It is up to the coming generations to run with the baton.

Follow me on Facebook or my web page to learn about the next family saga.

https://janeenannoconnell.com/
    https://www.facebook.com/JaneenAnnOConnell/
    Please contact me on:
    janeeno@outlook.com
    I look forward to hearing from you.

Book One of the Cullen / Bartlett Dynasty *"No Room for Regret"*
    Book Two – *Love, Lies and Legacies*
    Visit my website to order signed, author copies.

Future works:

My grandmother, Alice Alexandra Proctor's family, has stories full of adventure. From Norfolk in England, and Ayrshire in Scotland, to the gold fields of Victoria. Building empires in Lancefield and Kyabram in country Victoria, and in far north Queensland. The families left significant impressions politically as well as socially.

Their voices want to be heard.

NOTES

4. Betsy

1. A post office **opened** at Hobart in 1809. In 1812 John Beaumont was appointed as postmaster. In 1832 the post office became a government department and John Collicott was appointed as the first Postmaster-General in 1834.
(www.naa.gov.au/collection/fact-sheets/fs50.aspx)
2. The British Transportation Act confirmed the legal basis for assignment and from 1826 the Superintendent of Police decided the allocation of convicts until a local Assignment Board was established in 1832. (www.parliament.tas.gov.au)
3. *Melbourne c 1840 https://poi-australia.com.au/melbourne-in-the-1840s/>*

6. Betsy

1. https://poi-australia.com.au/melbourne-in-the-1840s/

8. Catherine

1. The Courier (Hobart Tas) 24 November 1840 p.2 Shipping Intelligence (www.trove.nla.gov.au)

9. William and Margaret

1. *Launceston Advertiser,* Thursday 18th March 1841, page 3. (www.trove.nla.gov.au
2. The Courier, Hobart.24 September 1841, p4 (www.trove.nla.gov.au)

11. William

1. John Blay is on the Census for Port Phillip, Bourke, 1841. He is listed as living in a stone building.

12. Families

1. **Author's note:** According to Elizabeth Blay's (nee Fogarty) obituary, she had fourteen children. I can find registrations for thirteen. The assumption of

genealogy is that one birth was not registered. At the time of this setting, still-births were often not registered. So I have used creative licence.

13. William's new start

1. Graphic from Greensborough Historical Society

14. Greenhills, River Plenty

1. Port Phillip Patriot and Melbourne Advertiser 20 July 1840. (trove.nla.gov.au)
2. Ancestry.com.au

16. Collingwood

1. "Tens of thousands of rural households made their own candles by pouring fat into a metal mould. Like so many of the simple manufacturing tasks, it was open to error. If the fat was heated incorrectly, the candle did not burn effectively."
   Geoffrey Blainey *Black Kettle and Full Moon. Daily Life in a Vanished Australia*, p. 47. Penguin Australia, 2003.
2. Port Phillip Gazette and Settler's Journal 24 December 1845 page 2. (trove.nla.gov.au)

19. William

1. Public Records Office, Victoria.
2. www.heraldsun.com.au/news/victoria/victorian-psychiatric-patients-grim-fate-in-hellish-1800s-hospitals/news-story
3. Public Records Office, Victoria.
4. Public Records Office, Victoria.

22. Margaret

1. Author's note: PROV advise that there is no coroner's inquest report, nor was a death certificate raised..

25. Elizabeth

1. Tasmanian Archives and Heritage Office. **NOTE** – Susanna has called herself Elizabeth on the marriage certificate.

26. Elizabeth Blay

1. Trove.nla.gov.au
2. The Argus 25 August 1862. Page 4 (trove.nla.gov.au)
3. Victoria, Australia, Rate Books 1855-1963. Public Records Office, Victoria.
4. New South Wales, Australia, Assisted Immigrant Passenger Lists, 1828-1896

28. Elizabeth Blay (nee Fogarty)

1. Victorian BDM. Registration number 4441

32. Margaret

1. Public Record Office Victoria; North Melbourne, Australia; Series Title: 2336/P Microfilm copy of Rate Books, City of Fitzroy [copy of VPRS 4301] [1858-1901]
2. <https://ozvta.files.wordpress.com/2011/01/1867-2772016.pdf>

33. Elizabeth

1. Public Records Office, Victoria

35. Elizabeth

1. Australia, City Directories, 1845-1948
2. The Age 14 May 1872, page 3. (trove.nla.gov.au)

37. Elizabeth

1. Vic. BDM death certificate. Registration number: 2429
2. St Kilda Cemetery, 1859 – 1987 – Ancestry.com.au
3. The Age. 9 February 1885 page 1. Family Notices. (Trove.nla.gov.au)

38. Margaret Frances McBeath

1. Australia, Electoral Rolls 1903-1980
2. Australia, Marriage Index, 1788-1950

39. Richard Werrett

1. Public Records Office, Victoria
2. The Argus 20 August 1860. Page 5. (Trove.nla.gov.au)

40. Mary Ann Werrett (nee Williams)

1. Port Phillip Patriot and Melbourne Advertiser 20 July 1840. (trove.nla.gov.au)

41. Richard Werrett

1. Public Records Office, Victoria

43. Charles

1. The Queen, Elizabeth II, bestowed the title "Royal" in 1958.

44. Margaret Frances Werrett (nee McBeath)

1. 1888, English, Book, Illustrated edition: The Jubilee history of Victoria and Melbourne, illustrated / T.W.H. Leavitt, editor; W.D. Lilburn, ... historian. https://trove.nla.gov.au/work/13186137
2. The Age 26 October 1906. (trove.nla.gov.au)
3. Electoral Rolls – Ancestry.com.au
4. The Argus 21 November 1910 (trove.nla.gov.au)
5. The Argus 11 Jan. 1812. (Trove.nla.gov.au)
6. Reporter (Box Hill) 2 August 1912 (Trove.nla.gov.au)

45. The First World War

1. naa.gov.au (National Archives of Australia)
2. From family collection
3. 22nd Australian Infantry Battalion (source:www.awm.gov.au/unit/U51462/)

46. Margaret Frances Werrett

1. Australian Dictionary of Biography, Volume 10, (MUP), 1986
2. The Argus 20 May 1918 (Trove.nla.gov.au)
3. National Archives of Australia (naa.gov.au)

47. Charles Mark Werrett

1. Public Records Office, Victoria (shipping list)
2. Claire Marie Leroux and Roland Mark Werrett (France). (Family photograph.)
3. Who's Who in Australia 1927. (Ancestry.com.au)

48. Margaret Frances Werrett (nee McBeath)

1. The Australasian 9 September 1922. (Trove.nla.gov.au)
2. The Argus 18 August 1923 (trove.nla.gov.au)
3. *The Australasian* 12 January 1924 page 33. (trove.nla.gov.au)
4. Trove.nla.gov.au

49. Hector Ralph Werrett

1. See end of book.

50. Sir William George McBeath

1. Delegates to the Geneva Convention, The Australasian, 25 October 1924, page 20. (trove.nla.gov.au
2. Trove.nla.gov.au
3. Trove.nla.gov.au
4. Trove.nla.gov.au
5. Trove.nla.gov.au
6. Sir William and Lady McBeath, National Library of Australia.
7. Record (Emerald Hill) 12 March 1927.
8. Trove.nla.gov.au

9 781034 454434